T0329193

# THE SIRIUS SQUAD: EARTH'S LAST DEFENCE

## By Khulekani Magubane

*Illustration by Luyanda Zindela*

*Photography by Lotte Manicom*

umSinsi Press
PO Box 28129
Malvern
4055
Kwa-Zulu Natal
South Africa
www.dancingpencils.co.za

ISBN 978-1-4309-0434-2

*This novel is original and all views expressed in the book reflect the Authors' beliefs. The opinions and views expressed are not those of **umSinsi Press**. We are an independent publishing company whose sacred objective is to provide budding authors with a platform from which their voices can be heard. We believe in publishing information and view-points of different cultures and from different perspectives, in fairness and recognition of our country's wonderful diversity.*

## Acknowledgements:

*To my father Z.E., my uncle Malume Somkhathi, my brother Nsika and my friend Clayton: Always missed, never forgotten.*

*To Larry, Lorna, Caryn, Miriam, Andriques and Lotte: Thanks for friendship, the inspiration and for listening to my senseless rambling.*

*To Luyanda for the cover art and for just being a champ.*

*Mom. You're one of a kind!*

# Contents

# PROLOGUE

*Location: Pantatma Village, Planet Gliese 581 G*

The red smoke from the vicious battle with the Mathra Empire was far from settling, even though the advanced galactic pirates took over the Gliese planet days before. The last Mathra warship left the day before but the damage and devastation was clear for all survivors to see, if any remained.

Huts lay demolished. Gardens that sustained the dedicated farmers were scorched beyond rehabilitation. The fires kept on as though there were still much left in the Pantatma village to destroy. But it was all in cinders and the High Guard of Andromeda was too late.

Taheeq's eyes scanned the dusty orange terrain of the Pantatma village, once renowned for its innovative horticulture. He slowly turned his head to the left and right as his glowing eyes dilated, searching for any survivors of the brutal siege.

Taheeq activated his communication device on the left shoulder pad of his armour. The device amplified his thought frequency and converted his thoughts into audible messages which could be heard almost immediately by those sporting paired devices.

"They were all destroyed. For no good reason other than that the Mathra needed to make a statement. The Pantatma village posed no threat. The Mathra knew this and they did not care. They wanted to show us that no one is safe. Nothing is sacred," his thoughts crackled on the device.

"We're dealing with tyrants of the worst kind here. We were too late. I don't know what would make them so bold as to attack a village of harmless farmers, but there you have it. None of us asked to be here, but we will need to stand our ground," Princess Innozia interjected from behind Taheeq.

Taheeq turned around and saw Innozia, the princess of the Andromeda Empire. She stood firm looking around at the damage to the village. Her no-nonsense scowl showed no pain. The wind blew the fine, golden, tentacle-like appendages on her head this way and that.

"You're right," Taheeq responded. "We should have never allowed the Mathra to become this bold, this strong. Now their rage has made them overly vengeful. Who knows? If the High Guard had just recognised their calls for self determination..." Taheeq stopped himself.

"Can we just perform the duties we came here for, cadet? I have no intention and no desire to debate the decisions of the Andromedan Parliament with you.

6

Not today. It's all a dead end in the face of more urgent matters anyway," Innozia snapped.

Taheeq raised his hands, indicating his decorous intentions. He knew raising any argument with an Andromedan was futile. They were naturally an autocratic, feisty people. They were also one of the most powerful empires in the entire universe, having colonised hundreds of planets.

Taheeq was far too mild mannered to retort to the Andromedan warrior princess, in any event. The heat in the Gliese star system was irritating Innozia's pale white skin enough as is. Taheeq admired Innozia's combative nature. He considered it refreshing, as most young royals of any intergalactic empire would rather be served hand and foot.

Taheeq was a Pleiadian. His planet was brought into the war against the Empire of Mathra, who were on a mission that had the potential to polarise every intergalactic convention and treaty of the past thirty millennia.

The Pleiadian race was an advanced species of hyper-intelligent, hairless beings with glowing blue skin. While they possessed formidable skills in battle, psychic abilities and, as one of the oldest intelligent beings in the universe, they had little to no pre-disposition for violence.

7

So peaceful is the Pleiadian race that they cannot even stand to quarrel. The two continued with other soldiers of the High Guard to search through the village for a clue that could lead them to the whereabouts of the Mathra ship which wreaked the devastation.

"Princess! Commander! I've found a survivor!" General Nammid shouted from a dome-like house that had been looted. Innozia and Taheeq quickly turned to the right where the Andromedan general Nammid was.

The forty two soldiers, from as many as eight different galaxies, ran to the dome where Nammid found the survivor. Innozia walked right passed her subordinate cadets, who waited outside. She walked straight into the hut.

She stood at the mouth of the igloo shaped structure then slowly walked in. She saw Nammid administering medicine to the dying native. His grey, scaly skin was slowly losing its glow, a sure sign that his life force was fading. A wound in his neck was fast oozing with black bodily fluid.

Innozia stooped down and looked at the native farmer in the face. His eyes constricted as he struggled to keep them open. She held his tendon like hand and tried to offer some comfort. She could feel his life energy fading.

"Please, sir. Tell us what happened. Tell us where the people who did this are. Where did they go? Please. We need to know," Princess Innozia pleaded with the dying farmer in her own language.

His voice croaked back in his own native tongue, a language Innozia and Nammid could not understand. Innozia's pitch black, salamander-like eyes dilated in shock and panic. The farmer kept speaking. She let out a frustrated huff. "I can't understand him," she said to Nammid.

"I can't get a word in either. It also doesn't sound like any language that's recognised by our commonwealth. And this region is not an ally of ours, so it's not likely anyone of our officers know his language," Nammid said.

Innozia's head hung for sheer frustration. "This can't be happening," she whispered to herself.

"None of us might understand his language, but I can understand his thoughts," said a voice at the door of the hut. Innozia and Nammid turned to the voice's direction. It was Taheeq.

"We'll think of something. Thank you. Please stand down," Innozia said bluntly. Nammid turned to Princess Innozia with a scowl of disbelief, but would not dare question the authority of her future queen. Taheeq remained standing at the mouth of the hut, his offer still extended.

"Cadet, you have your orders. Do you care to follow them?" Innozia insisted as she walked towards Taheeq. The Pleiadian stood his ground, not responding to Innozia's orders.

"Maybe we should try it, your highness?" Nammid interjected.

The suggestion stopped Innozia in her tracks as she was marching toward Taheeq. She turned around and looked at her most loyal soldier and best friend. "So you will allow this Pleiadian peasant to undermine me?" Innozia interrogated.

Nammid was quick to correct herself, looking downward the whole time. "Never, your highness! However, we are all aware of how important it is to find the Mathra Armada as soon as possible. And if this soul dies now, he dies with the key to finding the Mathra," Nammid pleaded while kneeling on one knee.

Innozia stopped to think about the proposition carefully. She could not think of any reason to refuse. She turned to Taheeq, her fully black eyes looked into his full-white glowing eyes. She sighed and motioned for Taheeq to enter the hut. Taheeq walked in thanking Innozia.

Taheeq passed Innozia on his way to Nammid, who was nursing the Gliese native lying on his bed. "And Taheeq," Innozia's voice called politely while he passed. Taheeq stopped and turned around to hear her out. "Don't ever undermine me again," Innozia cautioned.

Taheeq paused, slightly put off by Princess Innozia's apparent ingratitude. But being an unwavering soul, he continued toward the ailing elder farmer. Taheeq motioned to sit directly at the farmer's bedside. Nammid politely stepped aside and stood watching.

Taheeq sat and placed his left palm over the farmer's head and his right palm over his chest. He began mumbling a chant to himself repetitively. Innozia watched on, curious but skeptical. A wind began blowing inside the hut from out of nowhere.

The wind began howling even more violently than the wind outside did. Taheeq continued chanting to himself over and over again. He started glowing and the luminous blue light filled the entire room. Innozia and Nammid shielded their faces from the light.

The glow from Taheeq's body created a gentle whistling sound which filled the room. Almost as soon as he sat down next to the farmer, Taheeq's body returned to its normal appearance and he stood up again.

Nammid and Innozia walked towards him asking what he saw, heard or learned. Taheeq turned to them. While his perpetually vacant expression never gave away any emotion, it was clear that whatever Taheeq learned disturbed him.

"We need to leave this planet as soon as possible. We also need to help him, but he can't come with us. There is absolutely no time to lose," Taheeq hastened as he walked to the door of the hut. Taheeq motioned for medical personnel to be called in.

"Wait. What did he tell you?" Innozia said, dying to find out the truth. Taheeq looked down as if his worst fears were confirmed. Nammid and Innozia grew anxious to hear what he had learned.

"Taheeq, you're scaring us now," Nammid said.

"He told me that the people of this planet evacuated three days before the Mathra invaded. He is from a tribe on this planet that does not believe in leaving the soil of their birth. So he and others like him stayed...and they paid the price," Taheeq said clutching his fist.

"And the Mathra? What did they want here? Where did they go? Are they headed towards the Andromeda Parliament as we feared? Please, Taheeq, we need to know these things," Nammid urged the Pleiadian.

"The Mathra are not headed towards Andromeda. They're not strong enough to take the Andromedan Empire on as they are now. If they tried, half of the galactic authorities of the known universe would descend upon them. They know that," Taheeq clarified.

Nammid gave out a sigh of relief that her home galaxy was spared an invasion, if only temporarily. But Innozia needed more answers. "If they're not heading for my kingdom then where are they heading?" she asked.

"Like I said, they know that they cannot fight Andromeda on their own. They are looking for the positive Logos. They plan to use the positive Logos to build an army strong enough to destroy every last one of their enemies, almost effortlessly," Taheeq said.

Medical personnel walked into the hut and carried the farmer out. Innozia was even more confused. As a princess, warrior and elite soldier she hated feeling as if anyone knew more than she did. "If it's a long, complicated story, un-complicate it. I have all day," she insisted.

Taheeq looked back at Innozia. "At the beginning of the universe as we know it, there was a force known as the Logos. Whoever had the Logos had infinite power, allowing them to create or destroy anything, almost at will. It even gave its holder the power to manipulate reality itself.

"In their wisdom, a race of beings from the Sirius star system chose to split the Logos in two, so it would never fall into the wrong hands. They split it into the positive Logos and the negative Logos and placed each half on opposite ends of the universe," Taheeq said.

"Wait, Taheeq. It sounds like you're talking about something even bigger than our mission right now. Are you saying that it's more than Andromeda at risk right now? Are you saying that the Mathra have upped the stakes and put the whole universe on the line?" Innozia asked.

"Yes. For some reason, the Mathra have learnt of the Logos' power and want to use it against all of us and all of our home planets. This means that it is even more urgent that we find them," Taheeq responded.

Innozia began pacing about. "My mother told me about civilisations in the Sirius galaxy. She called them the Nommos. That's who they are, right? I don't know enough about them to say we have an ally in them. Would they side with us in this battle?"

"Yes, they are the Nommos. The Nommos are pure of heart," Taheeq said. "Like I said, it was up to

14

them to hide the positive and negative Logos. They've hidden it on a planet in the Sol star system. The Mathra are headed in that direction right now. Hopefully they won't find it soon enough..."

Innozia interrupted Taheeq, beside herself with the sudden complications to the mission. "Wait. Sol? Isn't that solar system a rural back-wood in the middle of nowhere? Nothing of any consequence ever happens there! I can't imagine that if this Logos is so important, they'd risk just putting it there!"

"Perhaps that was a good reason for the Nommos to hide the Logos there. It would be hiding in plain sight. The obvious thing to do would be to place it in the hands of a strong developed galaxy like Andromeda, or Taurus, or the Phoenix Cluster," Taheeq said.

"I don't see why the Nommos would have such reservations about entrusting the Logos in the hands of the most powerful army in the universe. Sounds like a better idea than leaving it in the hands of rural hicks who don't even have a galactic force," Innozia sneered.

"On the contrary," Taheeq argued. "They won't find the planet where the positive Logos is immediately, let alone the positive Logos itself. The Nommos were also wise enough to disguise it, so that it does not look the way that it always has."

"Let's not get sidetracked. We have a new mission right now. Taheeq, we need you to introduce us to the Nommos when we find them. Nammid, tell the soldiers that at sunrise tomorrow, we are now heading to Sirius and then to Sol," Innozia declared.

*Meanwhile on Nibiru, in the Sirius star system*

The seas of Nibiru ebbed as gently as they ever have. The silver shimmer of light from four suns, as well as the distant light from the colossal Canis Majoris, surrounded the water-covered planet. Nommos hunters and soldiers swam around the great sanctuary.

The sanctuary was the tallest building on the entire planet, and even its highest point was eight thousand meters under the surface of the planet's wall-to-wall oceans. The sanctuary's walls had the glow of polished marble. The marble had flowing curvy patterns. The buildings on the planet took on the same curvy shape.

Except for a small network of floating islands, the planet Nibiru had no land to walk on. Everything on the planet happened beneath its infinite oceans and Nibiru's people lived under the ocean their entire lives.

The intensity of the light on the surface from the stars was too great for the Nommos to withstand and they remained under surface of the ocean their entire lives.

Being a peaceful people, the Nommos never traveled outside of their own planet or star system for the purpose of conquest. As one of the oldest intelligent alien races anywhere in the universe, they were often charged with important assignments. Such a time had come again.

The Nommos Elder Amma gazed into her vision prism, a device she used to gain insights from beyond planet Nibiru. Sometimes it gave her insights from beyond the Sirius Star System itself. Her dismayed moans vibrated through the high council courts. Her servants knew she was not in a good way.

Amma was twenty feet tall and had grey skin. Her body structure had humanoid features with the exception that her legs joints bent to the back at a lower angle than human knees, allowing her greater ease of swimming.

She was hairless and had smooth grey skin, which made her resemble a dolphin. She was graceful under water. The other Nommos were the same height as an average human on earth and they took on distinct fish like features. However, they were also shape-shifters.

Two servants ran into Elder Amma's chambers after hearing her sonar waves of worry and distress. They stood at a glass wall that separated Elder Amma's chambers from the rest of the sanctuary. Amma was a divine being who nourished the Nommos with life and milk.

"Mother Amma. You sound distressed. Is there anything that our servants can do to assist or ease your discomfort?" asked a Nommos servant of high rank. He bent down on one knee at the floor of the sanctuary out of respect for the elder.

"Please call Mogoma. Call him to my chambers immediately," Elder Amma commanded. Without a word of concurrence, the Nommos servant swiftly swam out to find Mogoma and summon him to the elder.

Elder Amma began slowly floating in circles and spiraling upwards. The sonar waves from her moans and sighs made the entire court uneasy. The court's officials knew something was wrong. They had never seen or heard Amma so worried before.

Mogoma ran into Amma's chambers and stood straight, awaiting instruction. The six foot Nommos warrior was Elder Amma's most loyal servant, soldier and child. "Elder Amma. You called for me," Mogoma motioned.

Elder Amma looked down at Mogoma as she was floating. She descended and stood in front of the warrior. "Mogoma, it is time for you to return to the Sol star system. The Mathra know where the positive Logos is and they are coming after it as we speak."

Mogoma bowed his head. "I will prepare to take leave for Earth immediately. I will not allow the Mathra to get hold of the positive Logos. If I may ask, Elder, will we be getting any assistance in protecting the Logos from the Mathra?" Mogoma enquired.

"The High Guard of Andromeda are on the brink of declaring war against the Mathra. We will need to gain their trust in this fight. The Mathra are stronger, angrier and more determined than they have ever been before," Amma warned.

"And what of our child on earth? Clearly no one could have anticipated that we would need to fend off the Mathra this soon. Are we going to train him right in the midst of what could become the most devastating war the known universe has ever seen?" Mogoma asked.

"Mogoma, my child. We need as much help as we can get. He can help us find the positive Logos before the Mathra do. As for becoming a warrior, he will just have to learn fast. But you must find him as soon as you arrive," Elder Amma urged.

Mogoma nodded, knowing that he did not sign up for an easy feat. He stiffened his face and looked back up at Amma. "The Mathra will not have the victory." He bowed to Elder Amma and ran out of the chamber.

The Nommos servants had already placed his goods inside his spacecraft. The warp speed vessel was shaped like a swordfish and could travel through most known regions in the universe. But for now Mogoma just needed to get to earth. His mission was clear: make a warrior out of a boy and save the universe.

# CHAPTER 1: Time Suspension

*Location: Durban, Earth*

Waiting through time-suspension. That is what it felt like when Menzi stood in the financial aid queue at the Durban Institute for Humanities Engineering and Commerce. Standing in the queue for over ninety-eight minutes, he felt the nagging feeling he felt in other similar scenarios: that there was some other place he desperately, urgently needed to be.

He looked down at his application forms for the academic year ahead. He had enrolled for a Marine Biology, undergraduate degree. It was just the degree he wanted to study. Fortunately for Menzi, he could devote his entire day to registering.

Nothing demanded his attention or time at that exact moment. His manager at Jojo's Pizza showed uncharacteristic decency and allowed him a day off to register at the university. But Menzi was never the kind to question a good thing.

His parents were all the way in Richards Bay and, while ceased with the wellbeing of their son, were too preoccupied with their relative tranquility to be mindful of his current pains. It would not be polite to bother them with minor snags in any event.

Menzi had few friends and the only person he interacted with regularly in Durban, besides in bosses and lecturers, was his brother, Nathi. A thrifty blue collar entrepreneur, Nathi owned a chop shop dedicated to renovating and putting accessories on cars.

Other than that, Menzi's existence in Durban was quite a tame and mundane one. This made the sense of urgency in his gut all the more bizarre. He looked at the snaking queue behind him. He saw a line of lethargic would-be students ahead of him in the same queue.

Mlungisi, an obnoxious second year student, stood in front of him in the queue. Menzi knew Mlungisi most of his life, with their acquaintance dating back to high school. Everyone was in the queue to receive financial aid for their enrolment. More than half the hopefuls in the queue would apply unsuccessfully.

None of the students could afford to study at the institution, with the cheapest modules costing at least R40,000. Despite this, many of the students in the queue knew that they also did not fit the strictest criteria for a financial aid candidate under the institution's guidelines.

Mlungisi knew this well. He, like Menzi, came from a typical nuclear family with two parents who were both working and earned an income which was slightly above modest. But that is not what Mlungisi would tell the clerk at the end of the queue.

Mlungisi looked to convince the financial aid advisory board, as he did last year that he was being raised by his ailing grandmother. His mother died in a horrific taxi collision on her way back home from a late night shift and he knew nothing of his father except that he would have nothing to do with him.

Menzi did not hold Mlungisi's embellishment of his candidacy profile against him, although his unapologetic stance on the matter did irk him to some degree. Menzi decided that he would tell the truth about his family's financial position, regardless of how unfair he considered the strict criteria to be.

The sun's heat continued to beat down mercilessly on everyone in the auditorium, despite every doorway and window being left wide open. Menzi let out a broad yawn as he leaned against a large pillar he happened to be standing next to.

"Hey boy!" hissed a voice from behind him. He paid no attention, believing that it was not meant to grab his attention. Suddenly a hand with a firm grip grabbed his left shoulder and shook it violently. Visibly annoyed, Menzi turned around and saw a campus security guard standing behind him.

"What's this boy? What you smuggling here?"
The security guard obtruded as he pointed to the
inexplicable bump on Menzi's lower back. "Hey boy! I'm
talking to you. What are you smuggling in here?" the
security guard demanded.

"It's nothing. It's my back. It just looks like that,"
Menzi responded after he observed that the security
guard was referring to the bump in his back. The
security guard's right eyebrow cocked up with suspicion
written across his face.

"Unamanga wena! What is in here?" the security
guard pushed. He stepped closer to Menzi who turned
around and started stepping back. "I promise you sir. I
know it looks strange but it really is my back," he
insisted.

The whole scene grabbed the attention of the
other students in the queue. None of them thought to
assist as the situation escalated. The security guard
violently grabbed Menzi's forearm and twisted it,
pressing his face against the pillar he was leaning
against just a minute ago.

"Stop it! You're hurting me. I swear I'm not
smuggling drugs or whatever you think it is that I
have. I promise!" Menzi pleaded. But the security guard
would not hear any of it. He violently grabbed Menzi's
blue t-shirt and pulled it up.

He revealed a moist and scaly appendage protruding from Menzi's back, just as the young man said. Menzi groaned from the pain of his arm being twisted so violently. "Please, please let me go! It hurts," he strained, close to sobbing.

"Isilwane esinjani lesi (what kind of animal is this)?" the security guard whispered to himself as he walked away. Menzi looked back at the guard with resentment. He used his right hand to massage the pain away from his aching elbow. The security guard walked away without so much as an apology.

Menzi stooped down to pick his documents up from the ground. No one offered any assistance. However he could feel each glare on him after the embarrassing ordeal. No one ever provided him with an explanation for his fin-like appendage, or the slits on his clavicles, so Menzi never felt obligated to explain these to anyone curious enough to ask.

Menzi stood up again hugging his flip files and documents, almost as if he sought comfort from them. Mlungisi turned his head as his body continued to face forward. He settled on offering a pathetic "sorry, man" before turning to face forward again.

Menzi paid no mind to Mlungisi's empty apology. He looked through the flip-file he was carrying to make sure he had not lost any important documents during his undue interrogation. He flipped through four pages before he saw something that got him thinking.

He saw some old photos of his father visiting the Mopti region of Mali. His father loved astronomy, archeology and African history. His father told him of the journeys he took throughout the continent. It was, in fact, in Mali that Menzi's father met Elizabeth Wambui, Menzi's mother.

The queue had moved considerably after forty five minutes. Menzi saw Mlungisi running his game to the volunteer at the desk. She smiled dotingly at him as he harped out the made-up story of a dead-beat father and poor household headed by a woman too old to work.

Menzi rolled his eyes over as he watched Mlungisi wax lyrical. Menzi turned to his left and someone on the opposite end of the auditorium caught his eye. It was Zinhle, a girl he knew in high school.

Menzi did not know Zinhle well. They seldom had conversations in high school, but would mostly greet each other. Conversations with Zinhle that did last more than five minutes would leave Menzi cringing at how stupid he must have sounded to her.

She had changed a lot since those years. She wore stylish wide frame spectacles, a black and white striped formal shirt and a black skirt. She also had a dignified amount of make-up on, which was a no-no back in high school.

Menzi smiled at her as she spoke to someone from the administration office in charge of the registration process. She was four years ahead of him when they were in high school, so Menzi figured it likely that she had already graduated and started working.

Menzi saw how graceful was she even when in the middle of a mundane conversation. Zinhle eyes turned to Menzi's direction and saw him. Menzi hurriedly adjusted himself and looked forward, for fear that his ogling looked obvious and unsettling.

Menzi looked forward and dared not look to his right. He heard Zinhle laugh during the conversation. His paranoid mind began wondering if she was laughing at him. But it couldn't be. There was so much more happening in her immaculate existence, surely?

Menzi began shifting around to feign a pose that would allay any speculation that he had been paying the most intrusive attention to her. He almost missed the pillar behind him trying to lean back on it.

He settled for a putrid attempted at leaning with his elbow. It looked too rigid to be relaxed and he had already assumed the position too late anyway. He suddenly heard the click of Zinhle's stilettos. Each click sounded louder than the last. She was walking his way.

Menzi knew that there was nothing he could do to avert the encounter, although he suddenly became more self conscious. He assessed his breath and whiffed his armpits almost irrationally.

"Hello Menzi? Is that you?" Zinhle's voice said from behind Menzi. He slowly turned around, not sure what he would say once the conversation got started. Sure enough, Menzi fumbled as soon as his lips parted.

"Hello Zinhle. Fancy meeting you here! What a surprise. I did not expect to see you around here at all, you know," Menzi said as he nervously laughed at himself. Zinhle laughed back with a perplexed smile.

"Yes...well, maybe not because I just came by to make plans for the orientation week. So that's why I'm here. Anyway, how are you doing? Excited about your freshman year in varsity?" she asked.

"Yes. I'm in with marine biology. I'm very excited about what we'll be getting to do and I really can't see myself doing anything else..." Menzi said, just before stopping himself.

"It's okay. Don't spare my feelings. You should be here doing what you want to do. All the best," Zinhle said to spare the nervous freshman's anxiety.

"Although," Zinhle continued, "if you'd like to visit the Durban Observatory during our orientation week, I'd highly recommend it. It's really a different world when you're in that space looking up at the stars. I know, it's become like home for me," she said.

Menzi paused. An enthused smile broke on his face as he nodded. "Yes. Yes, that would be awesome. I'll make a point of putting that high on my orientation week *to do* list!" he gushed nervously.

The two laughed. "Okay, then. I can't wait to see you there. Oh, dear. It looks like it's finally your turn. Let me leave you to it then. Have an awesome day and all the best for the academic year," Zinhle said.

Menzi turned to look in front of him and, indeed, a volunteer was waiting to assist him. He turned to Zinhle and smiled. "Thanks. I'll take care of that and will keep in touch with you," he said.

Zinhle nodded politely with a smile and walked away. Menzi walked over to the desk where the volunteer was sitting. He pulled his backpack off and unzipped it; pulling out all the documents he needed for the application and proceeded to greet the volunteer.

"Good afternoon. My name is Menzi Gumede. I'm a first year student. I'm here to make an application for financial aid. Are you still able to help me?" Menzi asked as he introduced himself nervously.

"Sure," she replied as she took Menzi's documents from him. She paged through the documents and Menzi watched cringingly as she saw every single reason why he would not get the financial aid he needed.

Her eyes looked up at Menzi as she was still scanning the documents in her hand. He sighed. A smile broke on her face as she knew that Menzi was as anxious to get financial assistance as any undergraduate would be.

"I'm not even going to tell you that this is going to be difficult, if not impossible, for you. Both of your parents are still alive and earn salaries. Do you still want to go through with this?" she asked tactfully.

"Financial assistance should be accessible to anybody who cannot afford to pay for their studies themselves. I might have both parents alive and taking care of me. But they genuinely cannot afford to pay for my studies," Menzi insisted.

The volunteer sighed for sheer empathy and handed him an application form. He took the form with a polite word of thanks and proceeded to pull himself a chair and fill in the form on the table.

When Menzi finished filling in the form, he passed it to the volunteer and asked her when he would know if his application was successful or not. She took the form from him and told him to consider his application unsuccessful if he had not heard from them in twelve weeks.

Menzi sighed, frustrated that his effort and patience might have all been in vain. "Thank you. Have a great day," he said before standing up to leave the auditorium. The volunteer gave no response but continued funneling through paper work and application forms.

Menzi walked out of the auditorium's doors and looked up at the sky, the first time he was outdoors in hours. Even though he had just enrolled for the degree of his dreams at an acclaimed university with his boss's blessing, Menzi felt anxious.

He sighed, failing to shake the feeling that even though he had all his ducks in a row, something big was about to happen. There was something else he needed to prepare for. There was somewhere else he needed to be.

*Meanwhile, at the edge of the Sol star system*

The Mathra were closer than they had ever been to accomplishing their mission. The gigantic mother ship hovered menacingly on the edge of the Sol star system. Planets were mostly uninhabited and uninhabitable.

This gave the Mathra the benefit of stealth in their mission to find the positive Logos. This was not to say that the Mathra needed to hide from anyone on planet earth. Their armada was powerful enough to lay waste to every army on earth in a matter of days.

The Mathra had a clear and unilateral line of authority that allowed them to delegate functions and tasks. They were all led by an entity called the Architect. The Architect was a pre-evolved Mathrian which the other Mathrians served out of respect and loyalty.

The Architect planned the vengeance of his people for tens of thousands of years. He was served by high ranking Mathrians called Welders. Welders were the only Mathrians that were allowed to speak to the Architect directly. Only twelve Welders existed.

Another class of Mathrians formed part of the rank and file called Sculptors. Sculptors were the strategic nerve centre of the Mathrian Empire as well as plotting to do away with the current universe in order to give rise to a new one. Only two hundred Sculptors existed.

The final rank of the Mathra Empire was the Carpenters, a common class which often served as expendable foot soldiers, builders and servants. Carpenters easily numbered in the thousands. All ranks had the appearance of dark, anthropomorphic prawns but with slight differences in size and colour.

"Great Architect. We have located the positive Logos and will be able to have it in our possession soon. It is on the third planet from the star known as Sol," said a Welder kneeling before a capsule that the Architect stayed in permanently.

"Are there any identifiable threats on the planet?" the Architect's voice boomed from inside the large capsule.

"It is inhabited by a number of primitive beings, one of them moderately intelligent but completely unable to threaten our plans. The positive Logos is as good as ours and so is the entire universe," the Welder said.

"If nothing can stop us, then let nothing discourage us. Send the first warship. The people on this planet are divided. If any of them dare to challenge us, a united show of force from the Mathra will be their end," the Architect declared.

# CHAPTER 2: The Smoke Rises

*Just outside The Milky Way*

Taheeq sat still in a meditative state, legs crossed and arms raised straight up in the air. His luminous blue skin gave off a strong glow. Meditation orbs lying around him gave off more light in the psy-chamber, a room built to help advanced beings harness their telepathic or telekinetic abilities.

He drew in a deep breath as his eyes closed even tighter. The glow from his skin grew stronger, a sign that his energy levels were beginning to peak. His eyes opened wide and he found himself floating in the air on his home planet in the Pleiades star system.

However, it was not as peaceful and tranquil as he remembered it. The sky was on fire and the people were evacuating frantically, running for their lives. He stood still in their midst, slightly perplexed, wondering if this was real or if it was a vision from the future. A dark and sinister voice croaked behind him.

*"All things burst into flames and crumble into ashes. But the smoke...the smoke rises to the stars. It is inevitable. It is inevitable and beautiful. Young Pleiadian. Do you know what*

*you are seeing?"* the voice asked from just behind him.

Taheeq turned around. He saw a Mathrian loom tall and ominously behind him. He showed no signs of shock as the nine foot being stood in front of him. The Mathrian looked down at him with its glowing green eyes. Its black exoskeleton shimmered in the dark. Its face and head resembled that of a prawn with appendages protruding and large, emotionless eyes bulging out.

Taheeq levitated until he was at eye level with the Mathrian. His palms were raised to the level of his mid-torso, showing the Mathrian that he did not wish to fight but was prepared to defend himself if threatened.

"When will this happen? Is it happening already? Is the Mathra Empire behind all of this senseless destruction and suffering? What did the Pleiadian people do to deserve to meet such a cruel end?" Taheeq demanded of the Mathrian.

The Mathrian looked him straight in the eyes without making a sound. Taheeq stood his ground and demanded an answer. "What does the Empire of Mathra want to do once they have destroyed us all?"

The Mathrian swung a violent fist at Taheeq without warning. Taheeq blocked the punch with both arms but the force was so great it sent him flying into some rubble. Taheeq was not harmed once he hit the rubble and stood right back up.

Before the dust from Taheeq's crash landing could settle, the Mathrian charged at him to attack. At the last split second Taheeq managed to jump out of the way of the attack. As the Mathrian hit the rubble Taheeq counter attacked with a kick to its head.

The Mathrian went flying to another building which fell under the pressure. Rather than continue the attack, Taheeq waited to see what the Mathrian's next move would be. "Tell me what it is you want to do," Taheeq shouted.

Suddenly the Mathrian appeared above Taheeq. Taheeq looked up and saw the Mathrian ready to attack him. The Mathrian swiped at him with spinning kick which sent Taheeq flying to another building. The Mathrian's unrelenting attack continued as it pursued Taheeq.

Before Taheeq could get on both feet again, the Mathrian was right in front of him ready to continue its attack. The Mathrian began swiping at him with punches, each one stronger than the last. Taheeq managed to block or dodge each one.

Taheeq jumped up to the top of a building. He looked around and saw that he was in the city of Azot on his home planet in the Pleiadian star system. It was suddenly empty and all of the Pleiadians he saw minutes ago were gone without a trace.

Taheeq looked up. Somehow the sky seemed to be on fire. The fire from the sky seemed to be getting closer to the ground. A strong wind began to blow. Taheeq's garments swayed violently from the strength of the gust.

Taheeq looked straight forward and saw the Mathrian right in front of him, staring him straight in the face. Somehow Taheeq struggled to read its thoughts or even assess its spirit energy. It was almost as if the Mathrian did not even have a soul.

Taheeq was disturbed, but not afraid. The Mathrian stood motionless. As mild mannered as Taheeq was, he began to grow impatient with the reticent Mathrian. Taheeq flew at the Mathrian for an attack. He gave three good punches to the Mathrian in the torso.

The Mathrian seemed unfazed but Taheeq continued attacking. The Mathrian reached its long arms down to grab Taheeq but he retreated quickly. Taheeq grabbed the Mathrian's right leg and used all of his strength to swing it around.

The Mathrian seemed unfazed and Taheeq swung it around and around. Taheeq released his grip and sent the Mathrian flying to the ground at a blistering pace. Taheeq looked down bracing for a counter attack.

When the dust settled the Mathrian was standing motionless looking straight at Taheeq. There was no life in the creature's eyes. Taheeq's temper was tested like never before. He screamed for sheer frustration and flew down charging at the Mathrian. However, before Taheeq could make impact, the Mathrian disappeared again.

Taheeq looked left and right frantically for the Mathrian. However the Mathrian quickly snatched Taheeq from behind. It started running with Taheeq in its grasp. Taheeq tried to struggle out of the Mathrian's grip but all of his efforts were in vain.

The Mathrian eventually stopped running and slammed Taheeq on a cinderblock. It grabbed a piece of indestructible lyrudium piping, bent it and braced Taheeq's neck onto the cinderblock with it so he could not escape.

Taheeq grabbed the lyrudium pipe that was now pinning him to the cinderblock by his neck. He tried with all his might to pull it off of the cinderblock and free himself but it would not budge.

He looked up and the Mathrian was standing tall over him. Taheeq's frustration had reached boiling point. He was no longer willing to indulge the fight he found himself in. He demanded answers.

"Enough of this! I want to know what the pirates of Mathra are planning and I want to know now! Why was I shown this? My home planet. My city. Why am I seeing this? Is this the present or the future? Tell me! Tell me now!" Taheeq demanded.

The Mathrian stepped back and picked up the cinderblock it had pinned Taheeq to. It lifted him until he was making eye contact with it. It looked into his eyes breathing heavily. Taheeq knew his questions were about to get answered.

*"You puny Pleiadian! All things burst into flames and crumble into ashes. But the smoke rises to the stars. It emblazons all. It devours all. It becomes all. It is inevitable. It is inevitable and beautiful."* the Mathrian repeated.

Taheeq looked him in the eyes. "No more riddles. I want to know what it is you want to do. Surely if you want to destroy the home of the Pleiadians you would want to look one in the eye and tell them why," Taheeq insisted.

The Mathrian stepped back and looked to the burning sky. It drew in a long breath before it looked down at Taheeq again. Taheeq braced himself. Searching the thoughts of the Mathrian he knew that

he was about to get the answers to his questions. The
Mathrian started explaining.

*"For millennia we spent our existence as
runaway nomads, scaling the universe for peace
and freedom. The Andromedan Empire came and
took over our home planet tens of thousands of
years ago. They told us they were drawn to our
world because of the special solar energy from our
great star. They proposed to harvest this energy to
benefit of the Empire of Andromeda. The Mathra
took them on their word and allowed the
Andromedan Empire to build its stations and
refineries in our world.*

*Soon enough, peoples from the Empire of
Andromeda came to find residence on our planet.
No sooner than they moved into our world did
they begin taking unwelcome liberties. The
Andromedans began telling the Mathra on their
own land that they were unsightly and that they
disliked our appearance. The Mathra moved to
the swamps and wastelands of their own home
planet, all to appease those aliens from
Andromeda. The Andromedan forces on our
planet were too strong to oppose.*

*Soon the political situation on our planet
became too unwieldy for the Andromedan Empire
to control. Martyrs rose amongst us to demand
that we take our planet back by force. We*

marched to cities and towns that were taken over by Andromedan invaders. Naturally the Empire of Andromeda had a stronger army. Yet, more salvos still were sent from across the stars to wipe us out. We did not stand a chance. We lost hundreds of thousands in a matter of days. Those that were left chose to surrender, pleading for safe passage to leave the only planet we had known as a home.

For the hundreds of years that would follow we traveled through the stars like pathetic scavengers looking for a home. As you would already imagine, every planet that was close by was part of the expansive empire of Andromeda, whether as a colony or stronghold. We eventually settled for a star system with desert planets and large moons. I was but a child when this happened. I moved between twelve planets in my youth alone. Nothing got better. It was a pilgrimage from one hardship to the next. And with every planet that I called a temporary home the nature of the hardships changed.

And so did I. We became a nation of immigrants. No place was our home. But the place that we called home had been taken from us by parasites. Monsters. And yet they had the nerve to look at us as though we were the monsters! We have pled time and time again for our right to self-determination. We have tried to

*stress that our wish has never been the
destruction of Andromeda. But their drunkenness
on power has convinced them that to liberate us
would place them in a position of danger. We
were simply asking for our home back because we
have not been able to find another home since
they removed us from our own. The resources
were nowhere near as abundant as those on our
home planet; we lacked significant sustenance
and lived a hard life. We were oppressed,
disenfranchised, robbed and humiliated.*

*You ask me what the mission of the Mathra
is. The mission of every living Mathra is simple.
We will destroy the intergalactic order that is in
power in the universe. Planet Andromeda and
every filthy colony they have built from their ill
gotten power will be reduced to ashes. Every
people that benefited from the rule of Andromeda
will be nothing but a despised memory. All those
that were oppressed by the Andromedan Empire
and the like, but were too cowardly to fight it will
have their blood speckled across the galaxies. All
that will stand is a new universe. It will be a new
universal order under the supreme and
irreproachable rule of the Mathra. That is our
mission."*

Taheeq closed his eyes as he listened to the
Mathrian's account. He understood the rage of the
Mathra nation. He felt conflicted that he was enrolled

in the army of Andromeda and, by implication, obliged to defend a kingdom he personally found brutal and oppressive.

But he also knew that Mathra's blind rage and indiscriminate vengeance made them dangerous to innocent planets and peoples who had nothing to do with the once ruthless Andromedan colonisation.

"And this? Is what we see around us happening now or is it in the future? Please tell me. I need to know," Taheeq pleaded. The Mathrian drew his face nearer to that of Taheeq. It began to smell Taheeq as if to seek out any fear from him.

*"Why do you speak of a future? There is no future! We are already close to accomplishing our mission. We are seeking out the positive Logos in the Sol star system. Once we find it we will combine it with the negative Logos and have the power to destroy the entire universe and create a completely new one in a single breath. We are very aware that you are trying to stop us. You will not succeed. So everything you see before you right now is a certainty. But do not call it the future. It is an end. It is the end. It is the end of everything you hold dear. There will be no memory that the great Empire of Andromeda ever even existed. Or perhaps there will be. Perhaps their vile souls could be preserved in the shells of lesser beings which we could torture for all eternity. It is our*

*prerogative and none can stop us from
accomplishing our mission. Death is certain for
those who wish to try."*

Lights began to flash in Taheeq's eyes from all
around him. The light was so intense it almost blinded
him. Taheeq closed his eyes as he began to get
disorientated. When he found his bearings again,
Taheeq found himself standing where he was before.

Pleiadians were running from imminent danger
all around him. He looked up to the sky and it was still
on fire. He put his palms to his head and let out a
scream. The screams all around him were even louder.

"Taheeq!" Nammid shouted out as she shook
Taheeq out of his psy-trance. Taheeq woke up from his
psy-trance. He was back at the Andromedan space
vessel traveling to the Sirius star system.

"You were screaming, Taheeq. It was as if you
were having a nightmare, but you were sitting upright
with your eyes wide open. You were screaming as if you
saw a waking nightmare unfold right in front of you.
Are you okay?" Nammid asked.

Taheeq stood up and looked at Nammid. Taheeq
walked over to the window of the vessel and looked out
at the endless canvas of stars and galaxies. Nammid
followed him to the window.

"I apologise. I was tapping into the consciousness of one of the Mathra to understand why they are doing what they are doing. Now that I know the truth, I have to wonder if I am any better off for it," Taheeq said.

"Why? What did you see? What did you find out? If you're worried about anyone finding out, you have my assurance that I won't tell Princess Innozia," Nammid asked.

Nammid looked at Taheeq bewildered. Taheeq continued to look out into the abyss of stars and constellations, emotionless as usual. Nammid found Taheeq's words too worrying to ignore but too cryptic to truly understand.

"Taheeq? You know, even though we are in an army, we are still mortal and emotional beings. If you need to speak to someone about something that is bothering you I am always willing to listen," Nammid offered.

Taheeq continued looking out of the glass, motionless and apparently oblivious to Nammid's compassionate offer. Nammid thought it more appropriate to leave and give Taheeq an opportunity to think about the mission and his vision.

As she turned around she saw Taheeq again standing right in front of her looking her in the eye. She gasped briefly before she remembered that Taheeq had

45

the ability to create duplicates of himself when he was conflicted or deep in thought.

"Goodness, Taheeq! Could you just warn me when you're about to do that? Not all of us are telekinetic and telepathic, you know. In fact, it is against the Andromedan High Guard Protocol for soldiers to use exclusive abilities on duty," Nammid reprimanded.

Suddenly Nammid was surrounded by five semblances of Taheeq. They all looked directly at her and began walking closer to her. Nammid put her hands to her hips, visibly annoyed with Taheeq.

"I am starting to question whether I should even be a part of this army. So I need to know. The dark days of the Andromedan Empire's crusades across solar systems around the universe. Are those days over?" Taheeq interrogated.

Nammid drew in a breath, ready to retort, but suddenly stopped herself, at a loss for words. She sighed. "You know what Taheeq," Nammid started. "I really can't answer that question. Not now. All I know is this army is the only thing keeping the universe safe now."

Suddenly the other four semblances of Taheeq vanished and one was standing directly in front of Nammid. She gasped briefly. Taheeq looked Nammid deep in her pitch black eyes and touched her on her bright yellow face.

Nammid closed her eyes as Taheeq touched her. "You know I can never deny how special you are to me, Taheeq. But I am a soldier first and foremost. I can't leave. And if you leave, you'll have to do so without me," Nammid insisted.

"It's unfortunate that we can't answer these questions," Taheeq said. "We are fighting for peace, but we could get destroyed in the name of justice. And when that happens, who can we blame?" he asked.

# CHAPTER 3: The Mathra Strike

*Durban, South Africa, Earth*

Menzi's brother sent him to Musgrave to fetch his laptop from a store where he left it for repairs. He was still exhausted from a long day of doing nothing but standing around and waiting. He parked his old scooter outside in front of a coffee shop next door.

He was looking forward to getting the late errand done so he could go back to the apartment he shared with his brother where he could gather his thoughts and plan the year ahead.

Thoughts swirled around in his head about how he would fund his studies if he was turned down for financial aid. He wondered how he would balance studying full time and delivering pizzas.

He realised he hadn't thought things through as thoroughly as he originally thought. He was waiting at the internet café where Nathi left his laptop. Nathi was running the chop shop, where he never took a break even on public holidays.

He looked to the entrance of the internet café and saw a familiar face. It was Khosiano, a schoolmate that was one year ahead of him in high school. He had a single lens reflux camera hanging from his neck and a laptop bag slung over his right shoulder.

"Khosiano! How're you doing man! I haven't seen you in forever," Menzi exclaimed as he saw his old friend. Khosiano turned to him and smiled. Menzi stood up and the two shook hands.

"Fancy meeting you here. I thought I would probably bump into you on campus during registration. It got pretty hectic there a few minutes ago. I don't know if you saw it? There were cops and everything," Khosiano said.

"I was there a bit earlier than that. I managed to register for my course and submit an application for financial aid that I'm not terribly optimistic about. Police? Did students start protesting again?" Menzi asked.

"Yeah. The complaints are legitimate but the institution's leadership doesn't want to listen. And it doesn't help that the student reps are too scared of letting go of their benefits, so they're of no use to us anymore," Khosiano said.

"It's messed up. I don't know if anything can be done. I've kind of given up hope that anything will change, so this financial aid application had better work out. Did you register though?" Menzi asked.

"I did register for second year journalism. But I managed to get a freelancing gig with the Natal View newspaper. I'm thinking I might just drop out and try to prove myself to the news room until I get a permanent placement." Khosiano shrugged.

"Oh man. I wish I was at the point where I had a foot in the door like you. I can tell it's going to be a long year for me. I don't know how any first year student is going to get through it. There's too much against us," Menzi said.

"Pressure bro! That's what's going to change things. Have you seen the news? There are student protests in universities all over the country. And President Howard Hlongwane is expected to make a statement on it this afternoon," Khosiano said.

Menzi nodded. His political disillusion and indifference began to show. "I don't know if the leaders of the country are really interested in solving any real problems in this country. I always imagined that politicians had bigger issues to deal with," Menzi challenged.

The manager of the internet café emerged from the backroom with a laptop bag. "Menzi, the laptop is ready. Just tell your brother that when it asks him for a password he should just ignore it and sign in. It will work," the manager said as he passed Menzi the laptop.

Menzi took the laptop. Khosiano stepped forward to ask the manager if he could print some documents. Menzi told Khosiano that he would wait for him to get done and they could walk together. Khosiano gave a thumbs-up without looking at Menzi.

"I'm going to head to the newsroom in an hour's time. We can have some coffee next door and I'll let you know where all the hotspots are on your campus for Wi-Fi. Or we can just talk about something more interesting," Khosiano quipped with a witty smile.

After the printing was done the two walked out of the internet café and headed to the coffee shop next to it. They took their seats inside when they saw that the sky was getting darker.

"Gees, I thought it was supposed to be a bright day through and through. Well, if it's going to rain, I supposed this is even more reason to parley and have some coffee, right," Khosiano said.

Menzi shrugged as he sat down. "No arguments here," he concurred. Khosiano went to the counter of the coffee shop to order two tall cappuccinos. Menzi sat and looked out at Durban's South Beach in the distance.

Suddenly he noticed, from the distance, an object drawing closer to South beach. It was an object flying in the sky. He couldn't tell what it was but from the distance it looked dark and was shaped like a prawn. It moved in a perfectly straight line in the sky and stopped.

Khosiano emerged with two cappuccino flasks and noticed that Menzi was looking out into the distance. They both stood at the table wondering what the unidentified flying object was.

"If it were a jet or a plane of some kind, it would be moving, surely. That thing is just staying perfectly still in the air. What do you think it is, Khosiano?" Menzi wondered. Khosiano was stunned to silence.

People in the streets also stopped to look at the strange object in the distance. It loomed ominously over South Beach of Durban. No one seemed worried. Everyone was curious as to what they were looking at.

The object's altitude in the sky began to drop slightly as if it were descending. More and more people began to pay attention when the object started changing in colour. It would go from black, turn bright red as though it were set alight, then it would go deep purple, then black again.

People gasped and whispered to each other in awe. The object's alternations between colours got faster and faster. The sky suddenly darkened even further and lightning began pulsing between dark clouds without a single crack of thunder.

People began to panic and started seeking shelter. Khosiano and Menzi kept looking out at the object. It had not become an apparent possibility to anybody that the object could be related to the freakishly sudden change in weather.

Khosiano started filming the entire moment on his smart phone. He would take a few moments to put his phone away and pull out his SLR camera to take high quality pictures of people looking into the distance. Then he would pull his smart phone out and continue filming.

Suddenly a subtle but strong buzzing sound was heard all around the streets of Musgrave. Somehow the sound was fast escalating in its pitch. Menzi did not understand why, but he could not move his eyes off the object.

Musgrave went through a slight tremor that barely lasted longer than ten seconds. Suddenly a loud roar of thunder came from the skies. A beam of light descended from the flying object on the land around South Beach.

At least three explosions mushroomed in the central business district and the coast of Durban. People began to scream. Hysteria struck and people ran every which way. Those that were already in buildings and stores in Musgrave closed their doors and windows and others tried to run for cover.

Menzi looked around to see if there was any immediate threat in Musgrave. Menzi and Khosiano looked at each other with gutted expressions on their faces. They ran off from the coffee shop.

"Menzi, I need to be sure that you're going to be okay. I have to tell the newsroom and let them know how much I captured and then head off to where that explosion happened. I don't think I've seen anything like that before. Need a ride?" Khosiano offered.

"I'll be okay. Go ahead, my brother. My brother's chop shop was in that area of the city. I need to go there and find out if he's okay. You go ahead. I'll let you know what I find out. All the best and be careful," Menzi answered.

Khosiano ran to his bicycle and hurried to the Natal View newsroom. Menzi hurried over to his old scooter. After hopping on, he tried a few times to get it to start unsuccessfully.

He kept starting the scooter up with a twisted forearm almost as if so say the additional exerted pressure would force it to start running. It eventually started up and he headed directly for the central business district of Durban, where his brother would hopefully be waiting for him.

Menzi's scooter zipped past people running in the other direction or standing perfectly still watching the distant explosion, stunned to silence. The roads were in a state of bedlam as those in cars ignored streetlights to avoid imminent danger.

Despite the cars being trapped in bumper to bumper traffic, Menzi managed to use clear spots on the sidewalks of Durban city to get to the city centre where his brother was, hopefully, alive.

As he zipped past the Durban City Hall, he saw something from the corner of his eye that prompted him to stop. Menzi saw a pram standing stationary amongst the panicking crowd, but no one stopped to tend to it.

He moved closer to the pram and could not believe what he saw. Inside the pram was a little baby. Amidst all the mayhem, noise and chaos the baby was fast asleep with a peaceful, unassuming look on its soft, little face.

Menzi looked down at the baby, shocked and wondering how anyone would leave a defenseless infant by itself in such a situation. He immediately pulled himself together and took the baby out of the pram.

He looked around the pram for a name tag or a bag that might belong to the baby's parents but could not find one. He held the baby tight and continued running. The baby did not make a sound as people around them ran helter-skelter around it.

He ran past the City Hall and found himself mere minutes away from the building his brother was renting for his garage and body shop. He stopped immediately when he saw the whole building was taped off and demarcated by police.

# CHAPTER 4: Search for the lost Nommos

*Location: Earth*

Mogoma's spacecraft had been in earth's orbit for two hours before he could sense that a dark and powerful energy had struck the people of earth and devastated at least one major city. He had reached the site of his mission and time was of the essence.

He knew that he would have to move with great speed and urgency. But acting in haste without a plan was not the way of the Nommos. His spacecraft flew 19,500 feet in the air. He could see the margins of the planet's surface where sea met land.

He could even locate the home of the Dogon tribe in Mali. The Dogon tribe lived centuries ago and people of that tribe were the only civilisation on earth that knew of the Nommos alien race from the planet Nibiru in the Sirius Star system.

The Nommos taught the Dogon tribe their ancient wisdom and knowledge before the last of them left the earth. However, a few Nommos stayed behind to guide mankind but never kept contact with Nibiru. Most if not all were believed to be dead.

However, when Mogoma was last on planet earth he left a Nommos child behind in the care of a human family. This was the very same child that Mogoma needed to find urgently, if the war between the Mathra and the rest of the universe was to be averted.

Mogoma's spacecraft continued to descend in altitude until mountains and even large cities were distinguishable from where he was flying. He could make out the turmoil in the eastern coast at the bottom of Africa.

He could feel the fear, rage and uncertainty that had gripped the people living in that part of the world. He could also feel the darkness from the Mathra.

He also knew that the Mathra were not planning to do away with the entire planet until they had found the positive Logos. As he went over the horizon he saw a massive Mathra warship right in front of him.

The warship was colossal in its size, eight thousand feet wide and three thousand feet high. He turned his spacecraft around before the Mathra war craft could identify and target him. He knew that an early clash would be a losing one.

He about turned and started a steep decline. The land drew closer and closer to him as he descended. He flew over Durban and saw two large burning craters in the city. He now knew that the Mathra had struck.

He flew straight for the waters of the Indian Ocean and his spacecraft plunged in. He knew that the Mathra would not be able to find him while he was under water. He was also less likely to be discovered by human authorities and mistaken for the enemy.

Mogoma's spacecraft transformed almost immediately into a submarine like vessel with a dolphin like shape to it. Because Nibiru is almost entirely covered in water, Mogoma felt right at home suddenly.

He looked around at the sea life beneath the surface of the water. He saw sharks, dolphins, whales, fish, anemones, Portuguese Men-of-War, jellyfish. They floated around blissfully in their habitat, unaware of the danger their planet was in.

Mogoma turned the engine of his spacecraft off allowing it to float away from sight. His spacecraft landed on the bed of the ocean. He opened the spacecraft and swam out. His fin began to protrude from his back and the gills on the sides of his abdomen opened up.

His subtle scales already visible on his skin became harder and more visible. He swam underneath some rocks and boulders to find his way to a lagoon. He crawled out of the water and began scaling the walls of the lagoon.

Mogoma found a smooth patch on the wall of the lagoon. He placed a small device against the wall and pushed a button on it. Almost immediately, the small device started to unpack an array of accessories.

The device even erected lighting for Mogoma to see around the lagoon. Suddenly Mogoma had a large monitor in front of him, a resting place assembled and large pods with food. Mogoma walked to the large monitor screen and turned it on.

Elder Amma appeared on the screen. Mogoma would give her an update regarding his safe arrival to earth as well as the first strike by the Mathra on the planet. His fin receded, as did his scales and gills. Amma spoke to her child.

"Mogoma. I am relieved to see that you made it to your destination safely. Please do be careful. This will quite possibly be the most dangerous mission you have undertaken. Are the people of earth safe?" Elder Amma asked.

"They are still here, Elder Amma. The Mathra attacked. I do not know yet if the attack claimed any lives. Wishful thinking dictates that it was merely a warning shot. Warning the people of earth to surrender without a fight," Mogoma explained.

"Thank you for doing this, my child. We are here to help on every step of the way. More Nommos will be sent in time. But for now you know your mission. Find Kwataar, the Nommos child we left to serve as guardian of earth so many years ago," Amma said.

"As you wish, Elder Amma. I have not found him yet. But I believe he is out there. But he did not give out a signal for me to find him, which leads me to believe he does not know that I am here yet. I am not sure what to make of that," Mogoma said.

"You are absolutely right. We must find him soon. I must also tell you that the people of Andromeda have made contact with me. They say they will send their princess here to Nibiru to talk to discuss an alliance against the Mathra," Elder Amma said.

"Andromeda? The universally reviled colonists? That's interesting! Why do they need our help all of a sudden? Is the once mighty Andromedan Empire now so low on its knees that it must beg the Nommos for help?" Mogoma mocked.

"Mogoma, you know that we might not agree with the Andromedans but we have never been at war with them either," Elder Amma reminded.

"And why is that, Elder Amma? It's because we are a peaceful people as the Nommos. The Andromedans have built an entire empire from

61

depriving other peoples of what is theirs. They can say they are fighting to protect all life in the known universe, but the truth is they are just doing it for themselves," Mogoma politely asserted.

"Our misgivings aside, we will need all of the help we can get. We might not consider them as pure and good, but they have a place in this universe that is just as valid as ours is. We all have something at stake," Amma reasoned.

"I understand, Elder Amma. I am so sorry to second guess your wisdom. I will offer my assistance to the Andromedan High Guard when its fighters arrive here. I just hope that they do not come when it is too late," Mogoma recanted.

"Thank you my child. Please make sure that you find the child without any delay. Once you find the child the two of you must find the positive logos and bring it to Nibiru. We will safeguard it eternally from here," Elder Amma advised.

Mogoma bowed out of respect to Elder Amma. He turned off the monitor and left the lagoon. He swam out and up to the surface of the water. His head bobbed over the surface of the water and he saw that he was close to the shore.

He swam towards the land and saw that there were very few people on the shore. He saw that the few people on shore were looking out into the water. He made sure that all of his conspicuous traits were well hidden. His fins, gills and scales were hidden once again.

He began walking out of the water. The people on the beach were police, lifeguards and a few bystanders from the public. They stared at him, stunned with disbelief that anyone could have been swimming after the events of the day.

Civilians stared at Mogoma's tall stature and well built physique. His metallic pants were also a strange sight on someone who had just gone swimming. He looked around him, not daring to say a word.

"Excuse me sir. You're going to need to get off the beach. There was an emergency in the South Beach area and people are expected to stay away from the city centre and places of public gathering until further notice," a police officer said to him as he stepped out of the water.

Mogoma stared back the police officers with a blank expression. He turned and looked at the civilians behind the cordoning tape. He saw a lady standing with a small group grinning and waving at him. He thought it might be the Nommos he left on earth. After closer examination he knew it was not her.

"Sorry sir. Do you have any family and friends here? Perhaps you can find your way to them. We would suggest and, in fact, urge you to go home with them. It is not safe to be in the city or at the beach. We can assist you if you have any trouble finding them," the police officer continued.

Mogoma looked at the police officer again and then walked away from him. People were still mesmerised at seeing Mogoma. However, besides his nine foot stature and his near perfect muscular build he did not look alien at all.

"Oh my word, he's so cute," the lady that waved at him whispered to some people next to her. Mogoma stepped over the cordoning tape and walked into the streets of the North Beach of Durban.

His living garments formed a one piece metallic suit to cover his torso. A hood also formed to cover his bald head. He saw crowds moving away in an orderly fashion and single file. He merely followed in their direction, hoping they would bring him closer to Kwataar.

He walked past a hotel that was housing people after the blast in South Beach. He stopped and saw the large group of people at the hotel's reception area. The people's eyes were fixed on the television in the reception area.

Mogoma went over to see what they were looking at. They were watching a man speaking on television. He recognised the language because the ancient Nommos that visited earth thousands of years before were an intricate part of language formation, though little evidence of their presence and existence remained.

The man on the screen was the president of South Africa, Howard Hlongwane. He was addressing the nation on the mysterious blast which occurred near the south of Durban. He stood at a podium decorated with the South African coat of arms.

President Hlongwane's face was fixed with confusion, fear and consternation. He spoke slowly and decisively, careful not to let any flint of uncertainty show. He had no answers to any of the burning questions people had, and just as well, it was an emergency national address and not a press conference.

Mogoma looked on and saw that the leader of the nation was scared. He could not help but wonder how scared the nation must be if its leader looked so shaken and unsure.

"We are strong and united as a nation and we are prepared to tackle any challenge that threatens us. The causes for the explosion witnessed in south Durban are being investigated.

"Until state security and the security cluster are able to shed more light on the matter, we urge all South Africans to follow the instructions of the authorities deployed on the ground and to be patient as investigations continue," Mr Hlongwane said.

Mogoma heard the people around him groan and sigh out of frustration. A burly man with grey hair and red, sun-burnt skin stood next to him and was especially vocal about his dissatisfaction with the statement.

"Something like this happens and you really get to see the quality of leadership you have in a country, neh? We need real leadership," the man said.

Mogoma looked at him as he spoke but gave no reaction, not even a non-verbal one. People began whispering and talking amongst themselves, mostly vocalising their unanswered questions. Mogoma turned back to the screen.

"The authorities are still collecting reports of missing persons in the area, in an effort to recover any possible survivors of the explosion," Mr Hlongwane said.

Mogoma heard sighs of relief. Whispers and murmurs of uncertainty still floated among the people in the reception area. But Mogoma got the information he needed to get. No fatalities were reported by the authorities.

This meant that there was a more than fair chance that Kwataar was alive. This solved only one problem. Mogoma now needed to find Kwataar. It worried Mogoma that Kwataar made no attempt to be found since Mogoma arrived on the planet.

This led Mogoma to believe that Kwataar had either been captured or had forgotten his entire Nommos lineage.

Mogoma needed to get away from the noise and hysteria of the hotel reception room. People continued to grumble and complain about President Hlongwane, no different to the things they had to say about him throughout the rest of his term.

"As usual, nothing but spin! No answers, no clarity, no certainty! We need to find someone that can actually help us in this crisis," complained an old lady sitting next to Mogoma at the reception area.

"Don't worry. That's exactly what I will do," said Mogoma as he walked out of the building.

# CHAPTER 5: Discovery

*Location: Durban, South Africa*

Menzi stood on the corner of Point Road and
Main Street dazed and confused as civilians panicked
around him. He held the baby he found abandoned in
the streets just over an hour ago in his arms. His
foremost thought was finding his brother.

He was standing outside the apartment building
where he and his brother lived, yellow tape restricting
him from entering. Metro Cops, police officers, public
order officers as well as officers at a provincial and
national level were moving about calming the panic.

"We have the situation under control. Please do
not panic. Follow our instructions and you will be fine!
Please stay put and we will take you to a place of
safety. Do not go looking for your loved ones alone.

"I repeat: do not go looking for your loved ones
alone," pleaded a police officer trying to calm the crowd
as a woman sobbed in front of him, pleading to find her
child.

The red smoke continued to rise from the sites of
the two explosions that caused the chaos. The smoke
had a tinge to it that appeared to be of another world.

The smoke seemed to rise endlessly as Menzi looked to the sky and tried to track where it dispersed into air.

City centre taxis volunteered their vehicles in an effort by the authorities to get people away from danger. A police officer walked up to Menzi as he looked up to the sky, somewhat contemplative but somewhat mesmerised.

"Young man, are you looking for someone here?" the police officer asked bluntly. Menzi turned to the police officer as his face twisted from a vacant stare to a gasp of anxious anticipation.

"Yes. I'm looking for Nkosinathi. He's my older brother. Have you found him? Is he alive? Please tell me he's okay," Menzi fumbled, not even sure if he was giving enough details. His legs started to bend and jolt incoherently from his anxiety.

"Relax sir. I'm just going to check with the other officers who have been finding people since the explosion. But the good news is that they have not found any fatalities so there is a-more-than-good chance that he is still alive wherever he is," the officer reassured Menzi.

Menzi's breathing quickened, as his hopes were raised. He wanted to see his brother alive and well. The apartment building Menzi and Nathi lived in was partially hit by one of the explosions, which the authorities confirmed came from the object in the sky.

The officer tapped Menzi's arm and guided him in the direction of recovered survivors. Menzi went in the direction that the police officer, with his right arm, motioned to him. He walked past the yellow tape to enter the apartment building. As he entered he saw Nathi walking towards the door.

Menzi ran to Nathi and hugged him. The brothers held each other and started sobbing uncontrollably. Nathi's blue overall work suit which would usually be decorated by spots of oil, was covered in dust from rubble.

"I'm so glad you're okay, bro! I tried to call you and your phone didn't even ring. I was so scared!" Menzi panted as he released his brother from the long embrace to look down into his eyes. (Menzi was taller than his older brother.)

"Stop being a sulk bro. You see me, right? I'm just fine. You didn't see me panicking about you, did you? No. Do you know why? Because I knew that you were going to be okay." Nathi laughed off the ordeal, sarcastically of course.

Menzi laughed along with Nathi, although he was still shaking from the events of the day. A police officer called for attention in the lobby of the apartment building. She was a high ranking emergency operation coordinator with a commanding pitch to her voice.

"Everyone, please listen up. We are going to move you from this building to another place of safety within the next few minutes. You will get on the coach buses we have organised in an orderly fashion and from there we will be taking the first five groups of people to the Glenwood area.

"Many of you live in this building. It sustained considerable damage from the explosion and we cannot guarantee your safety if you continue to stay here. Apartments in the top three floors of the building have been destroyed. We are working to make sure we can provide an alternative to those who've lost property, but for now our number one priority is ensuring your safety," she explained.

Menzi turned to Nathi. Nathi looked back with a sad face. "The apartment was completely destroyed apparently. There's little, if any, chance of recovering anything at this point," Nathi explained.

"Yho...There's some much stuff I left up there that I still need! How are we going to replace it all? What does insurance have covered? Are they even going to cover a freak accident like this? Eish dade, ngiyazisa," Menzi said, vexed.

71

"Something tells me that is the least of our worries right now, buti. Right now we need to make sure that we're safe and try and get hold of ma and babayi. The officers are going to give us directions to where we're sleeping for the night any second," Nathi said.

Menzi and Nathi stood waiting for their orders. Menzi looked to the baby he was carrying in his arms. The baby was at peace, despite the chaos that surrounded them. But perhaps more peculiar than the child's serenity, to Menzi, was its appearance.

Menzi could not quite place the child in his preconceived notions of social categories. The child's skin was so pale it almost looked silver. The dark tinge in the baby's hair looked almost navy.

He also could not make out the baby's gender easily. None of this was particularly important at that moment. These were mere cursory questions that were running through Menzi's head that he thought he would have figured out by that time.

"You know we're still going to have to find that baby's parents, right? Wherever they are, I'm sure they're worried sick about their kid. It must be nerve wrecking to be separated from your loved ones in such a disaster, but a baby..." Nathi said.

Menzi turned to Nathi. Nathi looked back, slightly pained but with a glint of pride in his eyes over his brother's kindness to a baby to whom he owed nothing. Menzi gave a somber nod and held the baby even tighter.

The police officer who spoke to the crowd earlier began to assume a position to speak to the crowd again, carrying a voice projector. Nathi and Menzi turned their attention to her. She ran down the evacuation drill for the group.

"Alright people! This is what we're going to do. We are separating the group that is here into four parts. One of you will get onto a truck which will be coming momentarily to pick you up. The truck will take you to a facility in Queensbrugh. The second lot of you will get onto a bus we are providing for you to go to a facility in Pinetown. The third group will be collected by a bus which will take you to a facility that has been prepared for you in Stanger.

"The whole point of this exercise is to clear out the city and coastal areas. We will continue to clear out and evacuate the city centre and coastal areas over the next couple of days. If you have family members or loved ones you might be worried about, we will look for them and find them. In order to smooth out the process of reuniting you with any loved ones whose whereabouts are not currently known, we ask that you please, if possible, keep a form of identification with you at all times. For now, we would ask that you kindly comply with our orders and everyone should be safe," said the police officer.

Another police officer walked up to Menzi and Nathi. He pointed at the two of them, amongst others, motioning to count a portion of the crowd which would be separated from the rest and taken to one of the mentioned areas.

"You people get onto the bus that is waiting outside for you right now. Please keep to the group and do not follow any instructions except those that are given to you by law enforcement, police or the army," the police officer said.

Nathi and Menzi walked out with the rest of the crowd into the streets. Sure enough a coach bus was turning the corner and approaching them to take the group to a place of safety. Dark clouds began to gather over South Beach yet again. Menzi looked up.

# CHAPTER 6: *Menzi is Kwataar*

*Location: Durban, South Africa*

"Why do I have a bad feeling about those clouds up in the sky, Nathi?" Menzi asked. Nathi kept moving towards the bus. Menzi looked around as his mouth turned chalky. Menzi saw a queue in front of him, filled with people being guided into the bus.

His palms suddenly became sticky with sweat. He could not shake the uneasy apprehension that something bad was about to happen yet again. Cops shouted directions around him. Menzi gulped.

Nathi saw that his brother's frame of thought was drifting and got frustrated. "Come boet! Are you okay? We're going this way. What's wrong with you? Listen, we're going to be fine," Nathi pushed. Menzi momentarily snapped out of it.

"Nathi, I have a bad feeling about this whole situation. I don't think we should go with them," Menzi whispered to his brother. Nathi was slightly beside himself over his brother's seemingly ridiculous suggestion.

"Boet, listen. This is a major emergency. We can't just go on the fly and do our own thing. Especially now!

We can't disobey the authorities just because you have a bad feeling about stuff," Nathi said, shutting down Menzi's apprehension.

Menzi turned around. He looked around at other people preparing to be evacuated from the area. He did not see any uneasy tension to suggest that anyone else was as nervous as he was. He saw a police officer walk alongside a queue counting people.

His eyes were fixed on the police officer who kept walking and disappeared behind a pillar for a moment. Menzi's eyes blurred suddenly. He could hear a faint ringing in his head that could only be likened to concussion that he had had as a child, long ago.

Menzi's eyes began to ache. He closed his eyes and massaged his eyelids firmly with the thumb and index finger of his right hand. His eyes were so uncomfortable he could have sworn that they were changing in their structure right under his eyelids.

Menzi opened his eyes again. His vision came back into keen focus again. His vision was, in fact, clearer that it had been in years at that exact moment. He saw the police officer emerge from the pillar. But this time the police officer looked completely different.

The police officer did not even look human. He looked like an anthropomorphic crustacean. He changed form in Menzi's sight. He still had a human structure to

76

his posture, but had a black exoskeleton, much like that of a lobster.

Menzi gasped at what he saw. He looked around for anyone who had a similar reaction, but nobody looked in the direction of the police officer, much less stared at him. Menzi motioned to tell his brother what he just saw. But it was too late.

"Alright people! Let's move it. There's not much time to waste. We want to be done with this area to ensure maximum chances of safety for everyone in this area right now. This is not the only place we have to comb, you know," another officer demanded.

Before Menzi knew it, he was being rushed into a bus against his will. He held even tighter onto the baby he had found earlier in the day. The baby had not made a sound the entire time.

"Nathi, listen to me. I really don't think we're going to be okay here. I saw something before we got onto the bus. I don't like the feeling of this whole thing. We need to get out of here as soon as possible, boet," Menzi hissed in his brother's ear.

"Bro, can you please relax for a second! We're going to be fine. If you just stop panicking we're going to get all the help we need. This is not the time to be losing composure," Nathi retorted, visibly annoyed.

Menzi and Nathi sat down in the bus. Menzi began to restrain his worry, trying his best to dismiss it as irrational hysteria. He covered his mouth with his right palm, wondering if what he saw was some kind of hallucination.

The bus started chugging. There was surely no turning back now. Menzi had to trust now that what he was experiencing was his mind playing tricks on him. The bus began moving. A right turn off from Point Road was the sign of the bus's intention to leave the city.

Menzi looked around at the people in the bus with them. All of them were as confused as he was, but he was convinced that he was more scared than any of them. He looked forward and saw an armed soldier standing towards the front of the bus, watching over the passengers.

As he stared, the soldier's scanning glare turned to Menzi. Menzi immediately looked away, too scared of being caught staring. He peeked in the direction of the soldier again, out of sheer curiosity, to see whether the soldier was still looking at him.

Menzi slowly turned to the soldier only to realise that the soldier's glare did not leave him. He looked back and made eye contact with the soldier. But he noticed emptiness in the soldier's eyes as he looked back. It was almost as if the soldier did not have a soul.

Menzi tilted his head and constricted his eyes, genuinely confused at what was happening. The soldier's expression was vacant and his chiseled face was cold. Menzi was wondering if he was losing his mind. Suddenly the soldier started changing.

His skin was slowly getting replaced with what looked like a black, hard exoskeleton. His eyes began to gain a green glow to them. However, unlike last time, Menzi was not the only one who could see the unbelievable metamorphosis.

"Haaibo, Nkosi yami! Kwenze njani?" shouted someone from the back of the bus. People began to scream hysterically. Nathi also saw the transformation and was shocked beyond belief. "What the heck is going on?" shouted Nathi.

"It's that thing. I saw it before we got onto the bus. I thought my mind was playing tricks on me, but it's happening again. This thing! It's the exact same thing I saw before we got onto the bus," Menzi screamed.

The bus began to swerve left and right as the driver began to panic. People screamed in fear. The creature that was a human soldier just moments ago let out an imposing roar. One of the passengers, an elderly man ran at the creature with a small revolver he pulled out of his bathrobe.

The elderly man pointed the gun right at the creature and fired a shot. The creature was seemingly unfazed. It used one of its largest limbs, a long arm with a pincer like appendage to grab the man's forearm and dangle him in the air. The man almost immediately disintegrated into a type of soil before the passengers' eyes.

The screams got even louder as there was no doubt that their lives were at risk. The bus suddenly swerved and rammed into a streetlight. The passengers went helter-skelter, with some attempting to escape through the bus windows. Menzi froze as he looked at the horrific creature.

The creature again looked in Menzi's direction. It began walking to him, not turning its attention away from Menzi, even for a second. It raised its top and largest limps. The pincer like appendages at their ends turned into saber-like edges.

Menzi froze as the creature approached him. There was no doubt that the creature was pursuing Menzi as it stood directly in front of him. Menzi raised his hands yelling "no" as he clung to the baby in his arms.

Suddenly a bright light shone into the bus from the left. A loud blast disrupted the scene and the light blinded everyone for a few moments. As the light began to subside, Menzi slowly started opening his eyes. He was on his knees protecting the baby he carried.

As Menzi looked up he saw that the left side of the bus' body was completely blown off. Everyone in the bus was still alive. He looked up higher still. He saw a figure that looked like a man standing perfectly still in midair. The creature also looked up at the floating figure.

The brightness died and the figure became clearer. It was a tall bald man. He wore glowing armour that looked like nothing created on earth, except that it resembled the scales of a fish. The man looked down at the creature that terrorised the bus passengers.

Menzi looked up at the mysterious man that might have just saved his life. The stranger somehow looked familiar to him. The creature that was just about to attack Menzi looked up at the mysterious man and snarled in disdain at him.

The man's eyes went from having a pure blue glow in them to turning full black. The man slowly descended onto the bus until he was standing on the bus floor. He looked up into the eyes of the taller creature. Fearless and self-aware, he opened his mouth to speak.

"You have caused enough trouble to these innocent beings. You will retreat and I will spare your life. I don't wish to destroy you. This war can be won without the loss of another life. It need not even break out into a full on war. Walk away," the man said calmly.

The creature let out a strong roar which almost shook the ground. The few people that did not run away from the bus looked on in wonder. The creature stretched its arms up in a combative stance. It jumped up to prepare an attack on the mysterious man.

Without even blinking, the mysterious man drew a weapon from his armour and aimed it at the creature as it was in the air. He fired what sounded like thousands of glowing rounds in a few seconds. The creature's body suddenly flew back and hit the ground. Menzi was in awe.

The remaining passengers gasped at what they just saw. The man turned to Menzi and looked him right in the eyes. Menzi flinched and started moving back as he held the baby even tighter. The man stretched his hand out to Menzi.

Menzi did not respond. The man did not make a single move as his arm was still stretched out to help Menzi. "Kwataar. I have been waiting for you. There is no time to waste. You are coming with me," the man said in a deep, booming voice.

"I...I don't know who you're talking about. That is not me. My name is Menzi. I don't know who exactly you're looking for but it definitely isn't me. Thank you. I mean, no. I mean, sorry," Menzi fumbled, almost scared to look at the man in his eyes.

The man did not move an inch after Menzi's rebuff. "You do not know who you are. That does not change the fact that I need your help," the man insisted. The mysterious man started to glow.

Menzi was mesmerised by the glow that was coming out of the man's tall body. He reached out his hand to take the hand of the mysterious man. As he took the man's hand, Menzi could see firm scales emerge on his own arms, much like those on the man's arms.

The man helped Menzi up. Menzi turned around and looked to his brother. Nathi was still lying on the ground wondering what had just happened. Menzi turned to the mysterious man. The man understood what Menzi wanted to say and helped Nathi up as well.

"Like I said, we do not have any time to waste. We need to leave this place now before we are found out. I have built a hideout in a place where the Mathra will never find us. Your brother can come with us. Do not leave the infant behind," the man said.

"Wait. How did you know this man was my brother?" Menzi asked the mysterious man. The man did not respond. He walked in the direction of the area where the bus's passenger door once was. Menzi followed, carrying the baby in his arms. Nathi also followed.

Once all three of them were out of the bus, the mysterious man pointed to a vehicle half the size of the bus. It was a vehicle unlike anything Menzi had ever seen before. Menzi walked towards the vehicle and began inspecting it. It did not have any wheels, but it also did not have any obvious propeller mechanics or jet engines.

The man walked up to Menzi and smiled at him. Menzi smiled back politely. He did not know what to say next. The man reached into the neck of Menzi's shirt. Menzi was shocked but not afraid. He pulled out a necklace with a fish shaped pendant. Menzi had the necklace for as long as he could remember.

"It is so wonderful to see you once again, child of Nommos. You don't seem to remember anything. My name is Mogoma. I'm very sorry I had to leave you. But I am back now, Kwataar. It is time for us to fulfill the purpose we put you on this planet for," the man said.

"I'm sorry. I don't understand a word of what you're telling me right now. I'm so confused. You put me on this planet. No, my name is Menzi Gumede. I'm from Richards Bay. This is my brother Nathi. He knows," Menzi argued.

"Well you might have come under the care of some natives on this planet, but you are definitely not from this planet. You are from Nibiru. I saw you born there. I recognise you, even after all of these years. Let me show you," Mogoma said.

Mogoma motioned for Menzi to enter his vehicle. The vehicle changed its shape and took on the form of a platform and stairs. Mogoma motioned for Menzi and his brother to step onto the vehicle. "Or you can take your chances with the Mathra," Mogoma proposed.

Menzi and Nathi stepped into the vehicle. Mogoma stepped on after and the vehicle changed back to its original shape. Steering controls materialised in front of Mogoma. He started the vehicle and took the brothers to his secret hideout.

"You might be wondering what any of the strange things you might have witnessed today have to do with you. The truth is, it has everything to do with you," Mogoma explained.

The vehicle shot into the waters of the Durban coast.

# CHAPTER 7: Call to arms

*Location: Planet Nibiru*

Andromedan flight crafts already began their descent on the planet Nibiru. Their haste was clear as they scaled above the liquid surface of the planet at a blistering speed. The lights of the multiple stars in Nibiru's solar vicinity gave the water's surface an almost blinding shine.

The crafts had the famous cluster of floating islands on the planet well within their sights. They prepared for their slowdown and landing. The main Andromedan ship stayed just outside of Nibiru's orbit. Six smaller ships went into orbit to meet with the leader of the Nommos.

The six crafts landed on the largest of the thirty five floating islands. The foliage on the island was expansive, lush and untamed. They executed a perfectly synchronised landing on a mountain which was the highest peak of the island.

Princess Innozia stood up from her cockpit. She injected the chemical normaliser into her system. The device gave her body the gases and compounds her body needed to continue surviving in unfamiliar and dangerous atmospheres. Her craft opened up and she stepped outside.

As she walked out onto the wild cliff, she was met by her top ranking cadets. Nammid walked out of her craft and stood at attention to her captain and princess. Taheeq also exited his craft and stood ready to receive his orders.

Smeggar, a skilled warrior from the Orion Star System also stepped out of his craft. He stood loading his weapons as Princess Innozia approached him. The princess darted in his direction, ready to correct the Rigelian for overlooking her.

"Excuse me. Soldier, give me your name, rank and designation," Princess Innozia demanded. Smeggar did not acknowledge Innozia's presence, much less her order. He continued readying his weapons as though no one had even called for his attention.

"Soldier! You will come to attention in the presence of a superior officer or royalty! I just so happen to be both. Now give me your name, rank and designation," Princess Innozia raised her voice, visibly annoyed.

Smeggar turned around and saw Princess Innozia standing behind him, seething. He turned around slowly. Smeggar had a thick hide, similar to that of a grizzly bear. The hair on the crown of his head was longer, thicker and curlier than the hair on his body.

Smeggar was a behemoth of a being, more than twice Innozia's height. Smeggar squatted down to the point where he could get closer to making eye contact with the entitled princess. He looked Innozia in the face and huffed resentfully.

"Soldier. If you are not prepared to comply with my orders or give me your name, rank as well as your designation, I have no choice but to come to the determination that you must be disciplined. It's an extreme measure to take in these difficult times, but rest assured, if I am faced with insubordination, I will not hesitate," Innozia seethed.

Smeggar rose up straight and stood to attention. "The name is Smeggar from the Andromedan territory of Rigel. I have been assigned by the Rigelian Force to render my services in defense of the Andromedan Empire, and your honour, Princess Innozia," Smeggar sighed, reticently.

Innozia looked up at Smeggar, annoyed by his clear and poignant resentment towards her. She clicked her tongue at his attitude. Her fingers coiled as she fought off the urge to get into an altercation with the massive Rigelian.

"Malicious compliance is still malicious, cadet. I understand that varying narratives of history have had it that many of you do not see me as a hero, much less a superior of yours. But know this. I will not be disrespected on a mission that I am leading on behalf of my empire," Innozia snapped.

Innozia walked away from Smeggar, confident that she had gotten her point across. Other soldiers on the mission were perfectly quiet and still watching the moment of clear tension. As she walked away Smeggar responded to her.

"That's the one thing you don't understand, princess. Nobody is here for honour except for you and any soldiers who are naturalised to your empire. The vast majority of us are here because we are convinced that the success of this mission means the survival of our people.

"You might be on some ego trip because you get to pull rank and order people around. But what many of the soldiers in this group won't tell you is that we have no respect for you and no respect for the Andromedan Empire. We will work with you in defense of our worlds but we will never respect or recognise you as our princess," Smeggar said nonchalantly.

Innozia stopped in her stride away from Smeggar. She turned around to face him again. She walked sure and decisively in his direction again. She pulled her beam gun out of its holster and pointed it directly at Smeggar. Smeggar did not budge.

"Pride is a foolish disposition to indulge, young Rigelian. Pride without power is even more dangerous. You see me as proud, but I have more power than you ever could have. Your pride can only harm you because you have no power with which to back it up. You will be sorely humbled. Just ask your ancestors," Innozia said, striking a nerve with Smeggar.

"Not to break-up the team building exercise, but the leader of the Nommos is probably waiting for us to reach the shore of this island. Our work is urgent, so why don't we focus on that, regardless of how we feel about each other?" Taheeq asserted.

Smeggar and Innozia paused in their confrontational stances and looked at Taheeq. Innozia turned to Smeggar and pointed at him with a scowl on her face. "This isn't over, cadet. I will deal with you. Rest assured," she warned.

Innozia beat the path down the cliff and her soldiers, both loyal and indifferent, followed. The foliage on planet Nibiru's floating islands was fascinating, even for the advanced alien races in the Andromedan army.

The plants on the cliff took on a plethora of shapes and sizes. Some swayed in the wind like flying lanterns and others swelled and shrank as they took in and expelled the various gases of the planet's atmosphere.

Innozia and the cadets got to the shore of the island. The water on the shore had a liquefied solder alloy appearance to it. The Andromedan soldiers wore eyewear to protect them from the blinding light of the planet's atmosphere.

"Alright. Anyone know how we call up the person that calls the shots around here? We don't have any time to lose," Innozia demanded as she turned around and looked at her soldiers.

"That's how much respect she has for other civilisations. 'The person that calls the shots' she says. And she expects other people to respect her. She can go jump for all I care," Smeggar mumbled to another soldier next to him.

Innozia deliberately tried to ignore Smeggar's slights as she looked around for anyone who could assist her with contacting the leader of the Nommos. Taheeq stepped forward and volunteered his abilities.

"I can call out to the leader of the Nommos. Her name is Elder Amma. She is the maternal mother of every living Nommos. She is of ancient wisdom and practically immortal. It is important that we show her proper respect," Taheeq said to the soldiers.

The wind blew harder and the floating island began swinging side to side gently. Taheeq turned his back on the other soldiers and looked out to the waters. He raised his hands to the sky and his eyes turned bright white.

He started a chant which he repeated until the winds got stronger and stronger. He stopped chanting as the clouds gathered making the planet dark and cloudy. Still facing the water, Taheeq went down on one knee as if to bow before royalty.

"Everyone needs to get down on one knee. I can't stress how important it is to show the utmost respect to Elder Amma as she emerges from the water," Taheeq repeated himself. The soldiers complied with Taheeq's instructions and each went on one knee.

As the surface of the planet got dark the water turned from a shiny alloy to dark grey. Clouds began to stir in the planet's grey skies. Winds blew this way and that as the soldiers of the Andromedan Armada looked around, preparing themselves for anything.

The water made massive waves that crashed into each other. The island began to rock. Innozia and the others weaved their upper bodies left and right, trying to maintain their balance as the floating island buoyed violently.

A sliver sphere began to emerge from the waters. The sphere slowly rose from beneath the surface of the water until it was completely out of the sea and began floating in midair.

"That is the elder of the Nommos. She has chosen to honour our visit and to speak to us. Everyone, get down on your knees. We need to be as respectful as possible to this being," Taheeq explained with urgency.

"Wait. I don't understand. That thing coming out of the water is the elder? The elder of the Nommos people is a giant, grey flying ball? Nobody told me about this," Innozia shouted, competing with the howling wind to be heard.

"Please just do what I tell you to, Innozia. The last thing we want to do is anger one of the elder beings of the universe. It is quite likely that you have never been in the presence of a being this ancient. The elder is tens of thousands of years old," Taheeq pleaded.

All the soldiers in the Andromedan Armada quickly got on their knees so as not to offend the elder of the Nommos. The sphere was well above them but began descending until it was right in front of them on dry land.

The sphere began to clear up until the elder of the Nommos was clearly visible. She stood inside the large orb but was clearly taller than every member of the Andromedan Armada, including Smeggar.

She looked similar to a human woman but instead had grey skin like that of a dolphin. Her multidimensional consciousness hovered over her head, glowing to the point where it looked like a shining afro.

Her eyes had a blue glow to them that exuded great wisdom and compassion. She had smooth, fin-like structures on her forearms and lower legs. The only scales on her body were visible on her neck and shoulders.

"Please rise, children. Thank you so much for visiting my home planet. It is such a pleasure to see you all. However, we do not have a lot of time. The Mathra have already arrived on planet earth," the elder of the Nommos explained.

"Elder. Thank you for gracing us with your presence. We are here to pledge our allegiance to you and to the cause of saving the universe from the imminent threat of annihilation at the hands of the Mathra," Taheeq responded, still kneeling.

Innozia stood up and turned to Taheeq. "Is my soldier speaking out of turn again? I have a good mind to discipline you. The lot of you, in fact! I am the only thing standing between this universe and destruction, but you'd think I was a liability with the treatment I get from my own subordinates," she hissed.

Innozia turned to Elder Amma and looked right up at her face. She tried her hardest not to flinch at the elder being's size and imposing presence. Innozia looked into Elder Amma's eyes and saw nothing by grace, wisdom and purity. Innozia gulped.

"We need your help Amma. We have been pursuing the Mathra for a long time now. Any leads that you can give us as to where they are will be appreciated. And as the Princess of Andromeda, I am prepared to guarantee that you will be paid handsomely for helping," she explained.

"The only thing I covet, prize above all else, is the peace and stability of all of our worlds. The Mathra are on a planet known as earth in the Sol star system. That is also where the Logos is hidden. You cannot allow the Mathra to seize the Logos. With it, comes the power of creation and destruction itself. Once the Mathra get their hands on the Logos, everything we know will be wiped out completely as though it never existed," she said.

Innozia raised her arm to cover her face from Elder Amma's blinding light. She took two steps closer after the elder stopped speaking. Elder Amma went down on her knees and was still taller than Innozia.

She stooped down until she was making eye contact with her.

"Just one question. The Logos. Why did you entrust it to a planet of simple beings in the rural parts of the universe? Why did you not leave it in the hands of a power kingdom that could protect it from falling into the wrong hands?" Innozia asked.

"Innozia, you are not being polite! This is a supreme being, who lives in a dimension beyond our own. Her power and wisdom are beyond what we can even begin to fathom, and are certainly not to be questioned," Taheeq interjected.

Innozia turned around and scowled at Taheeq, confounded. "If you have forgotten, Taheeq, I am royalty where I come from. Calling me rude is not the most prudent display of manners either," Innozia retorted.

"Worry not, Taheeq. We have no time for pleasantries and niceties in any case. I am one of twelve fifth dimension beings that helped the Star Guardians create the Logos. One of the Star Guardians was separated from the others for trying to use the Logos for their own selfish ends," Elder Amma explained.

"I still don't get it. Why keep the Logos on a planet that cannot defend itself from a powerful onslaught. Why not leave the Logos in the hands of a powerful intergalactic empire, like... yes, I'll say it, the Andromedan Empire?" Innozia pressed.

"Because power does not equate to purity," Elder Amma explained. "We feared the power of the Logos even in our own hands, knowing the power that we already possessed. We knew that it would be best to hide it in plain sight among people who did not know how powerful and potentially dangerous it was," she continued.

Innozia shrugged almost as if to accept the circumstances as they were. "I would have done things differently, if it was me. No offense. What happens now? We go to earth and take the Mathra down, I suppose?" Innozia enquired.

"You are correct. But first you will have to go with some of my strongest soldiers. There are two Nommos on earth at the moment, but it is uncertain if they will be able to fight off the entire Mathra army. My soldiers will help you locate and identify the Logos," Elder Amma explained.

As Elder Amma spoke four hundred Nommos soldiers emerged from the water and started walking towards Innozia and her troops. Each one was tall but none was as tall as Elder Amma was. They were all either bald or had sparse styled hair on their heads.

"These are some of my finest soldiers. Do not worry if they are too few. Nommos can duplicate themselves multiple times if they are outnumbered in battle. They also know earth's geography very well," Elder Amma said.

"Be warned. The Mathra are very dangerous. They have limited psychic abilities and are masters at shape shifting and invisibility. However, they are averse to the water of the planet. If our plan has worked, the two Nommos already on earth have found the Positive Logos and all we need to do is keep it away from the Mathra," she continued.

Elder Amma opened her palm to reveal what looked like an old compass. She placed it in Innozia's hand. Elder Amma began descending back into the water. Her soldiers remained standing in front of the Andromedan army, ready and waiting to assist.

Innozia looked at the device and looked back up at Elder Amma. Through the Elder's telepathy, Innozia immediately knew that the device would help her locate the Nommos that were already on earth. "Understood. Thank you Elder. Soldiers, we have heard what the elder has told us. We are going to earth," Innozia declared.

# CHAPTER 8: Death from above

*Location: The Indian Ocean, near Durban, South Africa*

"So you're telling me that you saw me born and that I don't even come from this planet? That I am an alien? You understand why that sounds crazy, right? I can't be from outer space. My parents are both from here, on earth," Menzi challenged Mogoma.

"Reality is riddled with more craziness than even the wildest imagination, Kwataar. You will soon discover this. I don't expect you to believe me immediately, although I did not expect to find you suffering from amnesia. The truth will unfold as time goes by," said Mogoma as he sorted his tools against a cabinet, his back turned to Menzi.

Menzi stood and stared at Mogoma as he casually glided across his hidden lair, mystified by what he had just heard. "And that name, Kwataar. Why do you call me that? I don't even recognise it," Menzi asked.

"That was the name you were given at birth. It means 'messenger' in the language of the Nommos. The name was given to you by the Elder Amma, mother of the Nommos, as all of our names were," said Mogoma.

It was the morning after the explosion which devastated Durban's South Beach. Calm had returned to the city but South Beach was still very much off limits for anyone, including any person who lived there. No progress had been made by government on the cause of the blast.

Mogoma unwrapped the bands on his forearms, revealing shiny scales on his arms like those of a fish. Menzi's eyes dilated as he watched Mogoma. Menzi touched his own left forearm with his right hand. He felt them turn rough and scaly. He gasped and froze, looking at his forearm.

What shocked Menzi was not the appearance of scales on his forearms. It was encountering someone who had the same bizarre trait. Menzi was aware of his skin's ability and tendency to grow scaly since he was eleven years old.

Nathi, confused and afraid, chimed in. "Guys, this is getting very weird. If anyone could just come out from hiding in the corner anywhere with a hidden camera and say that everything that happened is a practical joke, that would be appreciated," Nathi said as he looked around at all the corners of the hideout.

"So if I'm not human, then why am I here? Why am I not on the planet you mentioned, where I come from, where I was born?" Menzi asked. Mogoma stopped what he was doing and turned to Menzi, still standing.

"You mean Nibiru? Well, look, we are Sirians, or Nommos. We are a race of beings from the planet Nibiru in the Sirius star system and we have been charged with protecting the positive Logos. You were assigned from birth the task of keeping safe the positive Logos," Mogoma explained.

"Well I did *not* get that memo," replied Menzi, his tone more serious than the retort seemed. Mogoma fixed his eyes on Menzi. He walked closer to him with a sure determined stride. Menzi noticed his change in pace and got nervous.

Mogoma kept walking until he was standing directly in front of Menzi. He pulled Menzi's mysterious necklace with the fish shaped pendant. "Look into my eyes," Mogoma demanded. Menzi looked up until he made eye contact with Mogoma.

Mogoma's eyes glowed bright yellow. Suddenly Menzi's memories began to rush at him, even those he did not recall having. He saw blinks and glimpses of a land that was strange but familiar. He saw images of an alien people that looked like him.

He saw glimpses of the baby he had just rescued on the day of the mysterious explosion. He saw the distant and looming threat of an evil more dreaded than anything he'd ever known.

The whole affair caused the entire room in the hidden lair to illuminate. The subtle ringing sound that accompanied the glow of Mogoma's eyes also grew quiet. Nathi looked around the room moments after in disbelief and fainted.

Menzi staggered backward and gasped. Breathing deeply he leaned against a nearby counter and looked to his right at nothing. His eyes were wide open with disbelief. His eyes had been opened. "Do you understand now?" Mogoma asked rhetorically.

"So this isn't even a baby? This is what those monsters are looking for? Why does it look like...? What do they want to do with it? And why am I supposed to devote my life to looking after it if the first time I saw it was yesterday?" Menzi inquired.

"The positive Logos is a mysterious thing indeed. It's not living but, on occasion, it functions as though it is. It can move, choose, think, even feel. Somehow, you and the positive Logos were separated after you arrived on the planet with it. It has obviously developed its own means of protecting itself," Mogoma explained.

"So I failed in my mission. The one thing I was born to do, I couldn't do, until an inanimate object I was duty bound to protect decided to wake up and disguise itself as a baby because I couldn't protect it? I had one job, one job! Are you sure you still want me on this mission?" Menzi huffed in self pity.

102

Menzi walked away from Mogoma and stood at the window of the lair, looking out at the sea life surrounding the lagoon. Mogoma followed and stood behind Menzi. He placed his hand on Menzi's shoulder.

"No one can choose a path like this for themselves. That is because no one can be competent or ready. It is thrust upon you and you are given no choice but to accept assignment and thrive," Mogoma said.

Menzi drew a deep breath. Mogoma patted Menzi on the shoulder and reminded him of the mission's urgency. "We need to find a way of looking out into the stars to get a sense of how close our allies and enemies are," he said.

"I think I know someone who can help us with that. Her name is Zinhle. She works at the city's space observatory. It has one of the most powerful telescopes around. She knows everything about outer space," said Menzi.

"Does she know about beings like me?" Mogoma asked, in a dry show of humour. Menzi's head dropped as he laughed to himself softly. "No Mogoma. I don't think she knows about beings like you," he replied.

Mogoma moved to pick Nathi up from the floor and carry him to his submarine craft. He began getting his weapons in preparation to leave the lagoon. Menzi followed Mogoma to the craft.

"We are going to need to find Zinhle and use her device to keep track of what is going on above us. We are in the very dangerous position of possessing the positive logos whilst we are overwhelmingly outnumbered," said Mogoma.

They got Nathi into the craft and entered it themselves. The craft slowly ascended to the surface of the water. As soon as it emerged at the surface the craft moved at a blistering speed. Menzi could see the glorious sunrise, a sign of hope in a dark time.

Menzi sat behind Mogoma in the craft as the Nommos warrior steered the vehicle. Menzi tilted his head to Mogoma's right. "Do you need any directions to get to the observatory?" Menzi offered.

"Not to worry. We are already on course to get there. The craft has already delved into your subconscious mind to get the directions, Kwataar. We should be there soon. Thank you for offering though," Mogoma declined with a smile.

Menzi was impressed and stunned to silence. Mogoma's calm and resourcefulness in the face of immense pressure made Menzi feel somewhat inadequate. Nathi began to wake up.

Menzi looked out at the sunrise again. In the corner of his eye, Menzi saw what looked like an elderly woman flying a certain distance behind Mogoma's craft. The woman's dress flapped violently under the wind's pressure. She wore large spectacles and her hair shivered in the velocity of flight.

Menzi looked forward again. A few moments later, after realising what he just saw, he quickly turned around again, shocked. He looked behind the craft and the elderly lady he saw moments before was gone.

Menzi wondered to himself if he was hallucinating when he saw the old lady flying behind the craft. Then he realised that he was in an alien's hover craft, looking for Zinhle as part of an elaborate mission to save the world. How strange can a flying granny possibly be compared to that?

The craft advanced to land within minutes. Before Menzi knew it, they were in the hills of South Ridge Durban, where the observatory and planetarium escaped as much of the city's lights and congestion as possible.

The craft found the observatory and executed a clean landing. Mogoma and Menzi hopped out of the craft. Nathi followed, carrying the positive Logos in his arms and patting it on the back as if to attempt to comfort or burp it.

To their surprise, the gates of the observatory were wide open and the lights were still on in one of the building's offices. Menzi walked to the front door of the building. He gave the door three polite knocks. Mogoma walked past Menzi and opened the door with no invitation.

Menzi stood at the doorway stunned as he watched Mogoma barge in. He didn't know whether to follow the Nommos or to try and stop him. Nathi also walked right past Menzi into the building. Menzi froze for a moment and reluctantly followed them in.

"That is not okay! I don't know how things are done on Nibiru, but you don't just walk into a person's place like that around here. It's dangerous and, actually, it's a bit rude. Not cool. Not cool at all," Menzi rebuked.

Mogoma turned his head left and right scanning the room for Zinhle. He paid no mind to Menzi's mild protest. Nathi paced around rocking the positive Logos in his arms as it started crying.

"Please keep him...it...quiet. We're trespassing right now and I don't know about you, but I don't look good in orange." The Logos was in the semblance of a crying baby.

"We might have more urgent matters to worry about if we don't act soon. I don't know if you understand much of what's happened over the past two days. I don't know if I even understand it. But I do understand that a lot is at stake," said a woman's voice from up the staircase.

Menzi turned around and looked up. It was Zinhle. Menzi's mouth turned to chalk as he saw her. She looked serious, pensive and worried. She continued walking down the stair case to meet with the three.

"Hello Menzi. I assume you're here to find out more about what happened in South Beach. Shouldn't you be at one of the safety camps? It's quite dangerous to be out there alone. Word is the president is declaring a curfew and anyone found after that curfew could be quarantined," Zinhle said.

Menzi gulped. He turned and looked at Mogoma, as if to call him forward to explain the situation. Mogoma walked up to Zinhle with a sure step. Zinhle stood firm and nodded lightly as a greeting to the Nommos.

"I take it you are Zinhle. It is an honour to meet you. I am told you have a device we can use to search the stars. We will need to make use of it because the world you know is in untold danger," said Mogoma.

"Yes. I have been looking out into the stars. It was the first place I thought of to look for answers to the questions of what happened yesterday. Looking at you, I imagine you know a lot more about it than I do. But whatever caused that explosion was not of this world. Am I right?" Zinhle inquired.

"Yes you are. The explosion came from a war ship belonging to an empire known as The Mathra. They are on earth in pursuit of that..." Mogoma said, pointing at the positive Logos.

"Once they get a hold of it they will use it as their ultimate weapon to destroy this and every other planet in existence," explained Mogoma.

"The baby?" Zinhle asked, mystified that Mogoma was pointing at Nathi carrying the positive Logos. Mogoma nodded. Zinhle walked up to Nathi as he carried the Logos. She reached her arms out, motioning to take the baby off his hands. She looked at it amazed.

"It looks like a baby. It's actually one half of the life force which created the universe and has the potential to destroy it. That's why the Mathra want it. We need to keep it from them," Mogoma explained.

"You do not need to worry about making sure that the Mathra do not get hold of the positive Logos. That is my job. All that will be required of you is to be gracious and stay out of my way," boomed a voice at the doorway.

Everyone turned to the doorway and saw an elderly woman waiting in the doorway. Everyone was stunned at what they saw. Menzi's mouth gaped open, as the elderly woman standing stalwartly in the doorway looked familiar.

"You...I saw you flying right behind us while we were on the way here! I thought I was imagining things. Look ma'am we're here on a very important mission and it's not safe for old ladies to be out alone at a time like this so..." Menzi started.

"I am anything but old and I am certainly not defenseless," the elderly lady interjected. She raised her walking stick and pointed it directly at Menzi. It transformed into a shining crescent scimitar with four blades each touching on their inverted sides.

Menzi raised his hands as his eyes dilated with shock. The elderly lady stepped into the house. Mogoma pulled a small blade from his combat pouch and looked directly at the elderly lady.

"Hey, Mogoma, you didn't tell me about this one. Is she a friend of yours? Cause if she is, then that's great. Then you can tell her I'm not a threat and she can stop pointing that thing at me. Right? Please tell me she's a friend?" Menzi stammered nervously.

"This is not an old lady. This is an advanced alien life form. It appears to be a shape shifting grey from the Zeta Reticuli star system. They are some of the most intelligent beings in the known universe. They have telepathic abilities and can even exist in multiple dimensions," Mogoma explained.

Mogoma and the Zeta Reticuli grey slowly circled each other in a tense standoff. Zinhle, Menzi and Nathi stood watching, motionless and too scared to move. The two immediately stopped moving and put away their weapons.

"What did I miss?" Menzi said, as he looked on confused.

"We've settled it. It was all a big misunderstanding. He is here for the same assistance that brought us here. Most importantly he is also dedicated to stopping the Mathra from getting their hands on the positive Logos," Mogoma explained.

Menzi jerked back and forth, confused by what had just happened. Mogoma and the Zeta Reticuli walked over to Zinhle and asked her to lead them to her study. Zinhle motioned for them to follow her up the staircase. Menzi and Nathi followed behind.

"We need urgent assistance to know where our allies and our enemies are beyond the stars. Is your technology able to help us in this?" Mogoma asked

Zinhle bluntly. Zinhle sat down at a stool and desk next to an electro telescope used to look into the stars.

"I don't know how technologically advanced your respective alien civilisations are, but given that you are able to travel to our planet and communicate with us, I imagine that our technology is considerably primitive compared to yours," Zinhle admitted.

"The best our technology can do in terms of looking into the stars is observing cosmic events. If you look into that telescope, most of what you will see is things that happened millions of years ago. It's literally like being in a museum," she continued.

"But here," Zinhle, qualified "is where we see that there are two major objects coming to earth from different directions. The reason we can see these, is because they are close and could reach us any day now."

# CHAPTER 9: Andromeda arrives

*Location: Over the Namib Desert area*

Mathra Carpenters space craft hovered over a desert plain ten thousand feet in the air. Small crowds from the areas of Walvis Bay and Sossusvlei gathered from a distance to watch the space craft in bewilderment and some in fear.

The Carpenters inside of the craft were surveying the desert area and the coast where a different Mathra assault craft fired a warning shot 1676 kilometers south east days ago. They began to establish contact with a distant mother ship where the Architect was waiting to give them their orders through the Sculptors and Welders.

The Mathra also began to notice an armada of navy ships advancing towards them from the Atlantic Ocean. They did not pay them much attention other than to verify that the ships were heading in their direction. Their potential threat to the Mathra mission would prove to be minimal.

One Carpenter began speaking on a monitor in the craft. On the monitor appeared two Sculptors and behind them stood the giant capsule which housed the Architect and leader of the Mathra.

*"Great Architect. We have tried the inhabitants of this planet. They are largely ill-equipped to face us in head on combat. If we advance with an attack on the entire planet immediately, the positive Logos will be ours in no time. If we can get the positive Logos before the Andromedan forces arrive, we cannot be defeated!"*

The Carpenters looked on as one of the Sculptors shrank from the screen and inched towards the Architect. The Sculptor whispered respectfully to the Architect something inaudible to the Carpenters on earth. They heard murmurs from the Architect also.

One of the Carpenters shifted the view to the navy ships floating in the Atlantic Ocean. None of them advanced to attack the Mathra ship. They floated out in the distance, almost as if to wait for a statement of intent from the Mathra before responding. *"Cowards,"* the Carpenter hissed to himself.

The Sculptor shifted back to viewing range of the monitor. The Carpenters looked on attentively. The Sculptor said nothing for several seconds. Instead it breathed heavily and slowly.

*"It is well understood that the positive Logos is within our grasp. There is no need to explain the significance of that fact. What the*

113

*Architect does not understand, Carpenters, is how, in the midst of your stay on this planet, with inferior defenses and primitive life forms, you allowed yourselves to lose a Mathrian when only one native life was taken,"* the Sculptor inquired.

The Carpenters froze. They knew that the Architect was talking about the Mathrian that was killed by Mogoma as it was about to attack Menzi and Nathi and take the positive Logos from them.

The Carpenters looked to each other, at a loss for what to tell their ruler. While the risk of being defeated by any forces already on earth was not high, the Mathra would not tolerate any eventualities that portrayed them as weak or compromised.

The Carpenters all knelt down and trembled when they realised that the Architect knew what happened. They made rapid clicking sounds as the quivered with fear. One of them built up the nerve to speak.

*"Great Architect! We did not at all mean to mislead you. There was just one death and nothing more than that. It was not even our idea for the attack to transpire the way that it did. It was a different craft entirely, which delegated its own orders,"* the Carpenter explained.

*"SILENCE!"* the Architect yelled.

The Carpenter stopped speaking immediately. The other Carpenters began to yelp quietly to themselves, knowing that the Architect was enraged. It was the first time the Carpenters heard the voice of the Architect that loud and audible.

*"Whilst you were doting over your superiority compared to the primitive beings on that planet, what you failed to consider was that you were not the only advanced being already on that planet searching for the positive Logos. Already a handful of beings capable of taking you on in battle are amongst you. Not only that, they are most likely in possession of the positive Logos as we speak. And to make matters worse, the Andromedan Empire has one large ship traveling to that very planet right now. Your procrastination and dilly dallying will place us on the cusp of a war we cannot win and I will not allow it!"* the Architect warned.

The Carpenters slowly began raise themselves up from the floor. They looked at each other and turned to the screen once again. They looked to each other again, almost as if to dare each other to speak to the Architect. One was brave enough to speak.

*"We apologise profusely, great Architect! It was not our intention to put the entire mission at risk. We will do whatever it takes to make sure*

*that we do not endanger the mission any further,"* the Carpenter pleaded.

The Sculptors and the Architect looked back at the Carpenters through the monitor, not saying a word. The Architect's reply was short and direct.

*"All things burst into flames and crumble into ashes. But the smoke rises to the stars. Destroy everything and everyone you can find. Show no mercy."*

*Location: Antarctica*

Andromeda's ship landed in the west peninsula of the Antarctic. Ivory mountains of icebergs stood in the freezing waters and smaller ones could be seen drifting and floating among them.

The door shaft of the ship opened up as the mist in the southern-most part of planet earth slowly crept in. Andromeda's soldiers walked out cautiously. They looked around at the snowy terrain.

Taheeq's vision allowed him to see more than the snow, icecaps and mist. It allowed him to look beyond what was visible to see the state of the environment that surrounded him. His face betrayed a sigh of sadness.

While Antarctica was one of the coldest places on the planet, he could feel an uneasy heat that told him that this part of the world was heating up faster than it would have naturally.

He could sense the discomfort in penguin rafts desperately looking for the sweet spot between thinning icecaps and waters that won't accommodate the fish they rely on for food.

"This planet is so bountiful and healthy. But she is wailing under the weight of her own children. As primitive as the beings on this planet are, they have somehow put this planet's ecosystem through its paces in a disproportionately short period of time," Taheeq discerned.

"Well, unfortunately it's more than just one small planet that is at stake right now and whether a group of mildly evolved apes are able to keep their own backyard clean is the least of our worries," Innozia interjected as she walked ahead from behind Taheeq.

"Alright soldiers. We are here. This is the big moment, the reason for our mission, the playoffs, the humdinger, the centerpiece. If it looks like we landed in a quiet part of town, that's a good thing. My strategists have advised me that the Mathra will be deterred from pursuing our base if it is in a low temperature environment surrounded by water.

"Also, the leaders of this planet have not established communication with us, so we do not know if they will meet us with hostility or receptiveness. What we need to focus on right now is finding the positive Logos and the Nommos that were sent here to help us," Princess Innozia explained.

"Well, it's obvious that it's not going to be that simple. As some point, we will get cornered and we're going to have to fight. What do we do when that happens? We're outnumbered at the moment and even if our reinforcements arrive the fight would probably be too big for this little planet to withstand," Smeggar asked.

An awkward silence came over the soldiers when they realised the true extent of the disadvantage they had in the fight. Some looked down. No one spoke for a few moments but the reality that this could be their last battle became all the more palpable.

"Okay, soldiers. Snap out of it. We knew that this was going to be hard, going in. Reinforcements will be on their way to this planet soon. Until then we need to make sure that we contain the situation. We won't be able to last against the Mathra Carpenters that are already here.

"Now, of course it would be foolish to expect the mission to go through without any kind of fallout, but the less contact we have with the Mathra at this point, the better our chances of securing the positive Logos and keeping it safe for a longer period of time," Innozia said.

"And if we do secure the positive Logos, where will the Andromedan Empire decide that is should be kept?" Smeggar asked. Everyone turned their heads to the Rigelian as he asked the questions audaciously.

"Will you trust the Nommos to safeguard it as they have for centuries or are you going to take it upon yourselves to become its next custodians? And can the universe trust the Andromedan Empire to be worthy guardians of the positive Logos?" he continued.

Innozia stared back at Smeggar, less annoyed than before with him, but increasingly weary and tiresome. She slowly walked up to the large Rigelian, looking him in the eye the entire time.

"I've said before that the Andromedan Empire is a worthiest custodian of the logos, if a worthy custodian in this universe exists. Your people might not appreciate those sentiments, but the cosmos is better for our empire's existence. It's better that way. And it's not up for negotiation or discussion. Understood, cadet?" Innozia seethed calmly.

Smeggar looked down and Innozia and huffed with contempt. "What most soldiers who serve the Andromedan army won't tell you is that aside from not

119

wanting this universe to be completely wiped out, you and the Mathra are just the same," Smeggar said.

Innozia turned her back to Smeggar and began walking away. "Your platitudes about my empire bore me. All that interests me is that you want the Mathra taken down as badly as I do. Let me know when you recall that and we can go ahead and do what we came here for," Innozia snapped.

She climbed onto her Andromedan rover vehicle and her top Andromedan cadets followed, boarding theirs. Smeggar walked towards his rover while staring at Innozia. Other cadets followed and they headed north, where the Mathra were waiting to give Andromeda and earth the fight of a lifetime.

# CHAPTER 10: *Sirius Squad*

*Location: Planet Earth*

*Washington*

The White House Briefing Room was packed to capacity with journalists and media houses from just about every continent. It was the most coveted press pass for any media house in the world, as the leader of the free world briefed the masses on the greatest threat to the world.

President Susan Bennett took her position at the podium. Her demeanor was authoritative and stern but calm and unshaken. She looked around at the briefing room, surveying the area, but did not fix her eyes on any of the reporters that looked back at her.

The American Navy had already been battered by the Mathra armada off the coast of Namibia and no word had been given on whether the United States would stand its ground against the strange new foes or retreat.

The world was waiting for an account of what had been happening over the past week from a global leader. The European Union, Great Britain, and other global superpowers were also readying their own statements and strategies. President Bennett spoke.

"Good afternoon everyone. I have just met with my National Security Council on the events of the past week. Firstly, it is important to acknowledge the hard work of Secretary Tolabi, Chairman Edwards and Admiral Schultz for the endless hours of work they have given our nation and the world on this matter. The White House is currently unable to provide any information on the nature of neither the threat nor the level of its seriousness.

"The army and our air force complement will be on standby if and when needed. For now we monitor the situation, as the intelligence we've received gives no suggestion that any attack or immediate threat to further American lives is imminent. The Navy will continue to stand ground. But a retreat at this point would be a betrayal, not only on those who we have already lost to this attack, but to America as a whole..."

*Beijing*

The General of the People's Liberation Army of China Li Huateng was not as gracious as the White House in the face of the extraterrestrial challenge. His stern face and impeccably assembled uniform was on every television screen in Beijing.

He was seated at his office at the Central Military Commission in Beijing, flanked by his second and third in command; however the camera in the commission's top floor office was focused on him.

People flooded sports bars, stayed behind the locked doors of their tiny high rise apartments and watched the top ranking officer of the largest army on earth brief them about the oddities taking place in China and around the world all at once.

"The People's Liberation Army has sighted flying objects off the south-eastern coast. Civilians have been evacuated completely from Hong Kong, Xiamen, Zhuhai, Shanghai and Hainan. Evacuation in the central regions is ongoing, although contact risk for civilians in these areas is relatively minimal. The People's Republic of China will not cower from this affront on its sovereignty and security.

"The People's Liberation Army is advancing to the south east to meet this threat where it has stood and not advanced since it became apparent. We are in communication with the Kremlin in Moscow, who have pledged their support for the People's Liberation Army. The People's Republic will not stand back, nor cower."

*Westville, Durban*

The South African government's camp filled up quickly as the news spread that the unidentified flying objects in the prime time news bulletins were beginning to attack people.

The government used the space in Westville to watch over residents of Durban who survived the recent events. Rumours began to spread that President Howard Hlongwane was preparing to announce a curfew, declare a national state of emergency and order that every South African found outside of a camp without authorisation be quarantined.

The atmosphere at the Durban camp, one of two hundred in KwaZulu Natal, was one of hysteria and a strange euphoria. In the crowded clamour some could be seen praying, others playing 1970 funk records and holding up signs which said: "Repent! Judgment day is upon us!" and others which read "welcome to earth" or "take me to your leader".

President Hlongwane had to address this crowd, update them on government's intervention into the problem and allay any fears that their lives were at risk as a result of a phenomenon which no government on earth knew enough about.

President Hlongwane sat in the back seat of a European sedan as it slowly drove through the crowd moving to heavily guarded location where he would give his speech to the people of Durban and, hopefully, ease any fears amongst them.

The tinted windows of the sedan hid him from the view of his people. This was not to hide the fact that it was the head of the state inside the vehicle. The conspicuous presence of the motor convoy betrayed the fact that someone of great importance was in the camp.

Sitting next to President Hlongwane was Themba Claassen, the head of the National Intelligence Unit, a largely covert and little known state squad devoted to spying and counter intelligence. If anyone in the country knew more about the current situation than President Hlongwane it was him.

"What we know from the side of the Americans is that they are thinking of pulling back. The problem with that is that they don't want it to be understood as surrender, what with the size of their military. But China and Russia are pushing ahead with an attack off the coast of Xiamen. People are worried this will force the hand of the Americans eventually. Nobody seems to agree on how to address the problem as far as the west goes. China and Russia are on the other extreme and nobody is expecting that to end well," Claassen explained.

Hlongwane nodded and gulped quietly to himself. He did not look at Claassen once. He reclined his head til his eyes were looking directly at the ceiling of the car. He sighed. He licked his lips briefly and hung his head again, straining in the effort to look his intelligence head in the eye.

"You want me to tell my people that we cannot fight for them because victory is impossible but that even if we retreat quietly our safety and security as a country is still at risk?" Hlongwane asked.

Claassen clutched the broadsheet newspaper he was holding in his right hand. He adjusted his pitch black shades with his left hand and after doing so reached his left hand over to pat the president on the shoulder.

"We are in a position where we can update South Africa without over committing and underperforming. If the Americans are thinking of pulling back all while China is pushing ahead, then you just know it would be crazy for us to try and fight. Besides, we are not the only country to have been attacked anymore. The responsibility does not fall squarely on us or you," Claassen reasoned.

The car stopped moving. Hlongwane knew well enough that it had arrived at the location where he was meant to address Durban based survivors of the mysterious attack as well as South Africa as a nation. He knew what to say to them but was not entirely sure if he believed it.

Hlongwane sighed again. He looked to Claassen and crooked his mouth to the right nervously. The door next to the president opened as he put on his signature sunglasses and stepped out. The crowd cheered as they saw their leader, albeit under testing circumstances.

He raised his hands greeting the people around him. Bodyguards stood in formation creating a human wall between the president and the crowd. Four guards walked ahead of President Hlongwane leading him to the podium where he would stand and address the country.

It would be his first official public address since an address from the Union Buildings. So much had changed since then. Reporters scrambled over the barricade partitions and over the shoulders of bodyguards to ask the president questions.

But this was not a press briefing. If it were, it would perhaps be the most disappointing press briefing by any South African government official in history. There would be no insight and questions would not be adequately answered, as not even the leader of the country knew what was going on.

Hlongwane walked up to the stage put together for his address. He stepped to a podium with the South African coat of arms on it. He stood still and looked at the crowd of people he was about to address. He saw tens of thousands looking to him for leadership and direction.

As far as he could see, there were people gathered to hear him speak. Even the hills in the distance that hid Queensburgh beyond Westville were speckled with crowds of people who were gathered at the camp after the fateful explosion.

*South Ridge Durban Observatory*

The shape shifting Zeta Reticuli explained to Menzi, Mogoma and Zinhle that he suspected that the Mathra's mission on earth was more sinister than the Nommos had previously feared.

"As it stands, we have no time to waste. We believe that they might want to abduct or even assassinate the leader of this country. They are growing frustrated because they did not expect it to be so difficult to seize the positive Logos," said the Zeta Reticuli shape shifter.

"What would that achieve?" asked Menzi. "And how can we stop them...sorry...I didn't get your name..." he continued, inquiring who the grey was.

"Name? Oh, yes. We greys don't have those. We are multiple embodiments of a singular being. My name is the same name that every other grey in the universe has. Zeta Reticuli," the grey explained.

"Oh..." Menzi responded awkwardly. "So, is it okay if I call you Zee? Cause not calling you anything is just going to be weird. Would you mind?" he suggested. The grey looked at him with a cold stare, as Menzi continued stammering until he resolved that silence was probably the best response to the grey's clarification.

"We must be very careful when dealing with the Mathra. They are scheming continuously and the only reason we greys know this is because we are able to intercept their thought waves, only to a limited extent," the grey explained.

"Are you saying that we need to find the president and stop the Mathra from assassinating him? When are they thinking doing this? How much time do we have to stop them?" Mogoma asked.

"They will most likely be plotting to assassinate or abduct him when the earliest opportunity presents itself. Right now they're watching him as he addresses the natives on this planet at a nearby hill.

"The decided purpose of the assassination is to draw us out, but we must stop them because, if they succeed, their actions will trigger a galactic diplomatic row that will put the mission of protecting the positive Logos in complete jeopardy," the grey answered.

"So you're suggesting that we go to them, even though the whole reason why they would want to attempt and assassination of President Hlongwane in the first place is to lure us towards them with the positive Logos?" Menzi asked, slightly put off by where the conversation was going.

"You catch on fast," the grey said as he turned his back to Menzi and walked out of the front door of the house. Zinhle looked as the grey walked out onto the veranda. "What's going on outside," Menzi asked.

"We've got company," the grey smiled. The grey looked up at the sky as a slight rumbling sound charged louder and louder around them. The small porcelain ornaments in the wall units and on the living room counter jittered uncontrollably as the rumbling got louder and more intense.

Mogoma walked out onto the veranda to see what was happening. Menzi and Zinhle followed him. The four of them looked up at the sky and saw small assault crafts landing in the front yard.

Menzi gulped loudly, the sound so audible in his own mind that it could only be overpowered by the loud humming of the yet unidentified flying objects landing right in front of him.

About three dozen assault craft began their slow decent to the ground. Each one looked like a flying motorbike with jet engines where the wheels should be. Menzi was mesmerised. Out of everything he had seen already, this most resembled a sci-fi thriller or that

130

film, Tron, he had watched years ago which he enjoyed so much.

He could not take his eyes off one of the life forms riding on the flying bikes. He could tell that this being was female. Her skin was pale with a slightly pink tone, making her look like an anthropomorphic swamp rose.

She opened her black beady eyes and flicked her hair like appendages from the front of her face. "Greetings! I am Princess Innozia of the great and mighty Andromedan Empire. I believe you have something that I am looking for," said the extraterrestrial being.

The grey smiled wisely as he saw the Andromedan troops. "Welcome Princess Innozia," the grey shouted. "We have what you are looking for. But the mission has gotten a lot more complicated than expected and we will need your help…"

# CHAPTER 11: *Earth under siege*

*Westville, Durban*

President Howard Hlongwane stood at the podium ready to give his address to the many survivors of the week's unbelievable events. He looked out to the crowd and saw many different expressions.

It was clear to him that not everyone was as afraid, unsure and doubtful as he was. Some smiled, oblivious to the potential danger that the country and the world was in. Others looked bewildered by the recent events but not scared. Others cried.

The diverse moods in the crowd emboldened President Hlongwane. He did not for a second doubt the urgency and seriousness of the situation his country found itself in. However, looking at the crowd of tens of thousands, he realised that the world was bigger than his fears. He raised his hands in the air. People cheered.

"Fellow South Africans. It is a privilege to stand before you today as a leader of such a diverse, courageous and resilient nation. I thank you for the faith you have placed in me at this difficult time. A lot has happened in the past few days that nobody can explain and even fewer can resolve," Hlongwane started.

The sun beat on his grey hair until his forehead and exposed scalp from a receding hairline had a shine to it. Wafts of smoke slowly rose from his scalp from the Vaseline and treatment gel and hovered above his head like a halo.

"The world is at a crossroads. The United States, with the most powerful military in the world, is contemplating a retreat; while China and Russia are pressing on to face the visitors. Very little is known about them, but it has been commonly accepted that they do not mean well, they are dangerous and they must be dealt with. We have our army ready to provide assistance to our people, but we will not engage in any combat without the support of our diplomatic partners in the international community.

"Our SADC partners are bringing soldiers in to support our efforts in keeping South Africans safe in camps while we find an alternative location for them at this time. There is no truth to the speculation that we are imposing a national curfew. We have yet to establish the number of people who are not in the safe confinement of a camp, and until that is established, it would be irresponsible of us to impose a de facto lockout on those who have not been found by the army.

"Until a plan has been developed, we humbly ask that you follow the instructions of the South African National Defence Force personnel. Do not separate from the core group of the camp you are in and do not try to establish any form of communication with the visitors on your own. But most of all we would like to leave you with the reassurance that we will prioritise, above all else, your safety and well being. Because...because...ehhh...because..."

President Hlongwane found himself staring at the sky mid-speech. The crowd looked up in the same direction as a large shadow cast itself over the entire gathering. A massive object flew over them before anyone even knew it.

President Hlongwane looked up at the gigantic object. It looked like a large scale, black lobster. A glowing green gas descended from the object and shimmered towards the crowd. The gas surrounded the president.

Everyone watched the flying object without making a single move. Hlongwane felt himself bound to stillness down to the marrow of his bones. He could not move. He stayed still in the position, standing head turned up, and mouth gaping wide open.

The object began to open up from underneath. The green lights could be seen glowing from within. Hlongwane stayed perfectly still. The only movement on his body was the subtle waving of his afro as the object blew wind this way and that and a small tear that fell from his eye as he stood motionless. Nobody could move.

Hlongwane could see a green light shoot out of the flying object in his direction. But he could do nothing to stop or avoid it. The green light flew at him like an arrow from a bow. It hit him and he suddenly regained the sense of motion again.

He flew back from the podium and landed a short distance from it, still on the stage. Suddenly everyone was able to move again. The crowd panicked and a stampede began to ensue. The president's bodyguards ran to the stage to attend to him.

The president was still alive, albeit shaken. The bodyguards rushed him to his vehicle and planned an exit route. As they picked the president up they noticed more of the flying objects from inside the larger one that first appeared, were approaching them. They made a run for it and pushed the president into his presidential sedan.

The car sped off and the flying objects chased after them. Suddenly rays of yellow light began shooting at the object pursuing the presidential convoy. It was the soldiers of the Andromedan Empire.

The main ship shifted its attention to the Andromedan soldiers. Menzi was on the back of the Nommos craft with Mogoma. He had the positive Logos nestled in his lap. It was the first time he got a close look at one of the Mathra ships.

The Andromedan soldiers continued shooting at the Mathra ships. As expected, the Mathra stopped pursuing President Hlongwane's vehicle and began chasing after the Andromedan soldiers.

As Mogoma turned his craft around to retreat Menzi got a good look at the visceral parts to the Mathra combat craft. It looked less like an advanced space travel vehicle or space age tank and more like a living organism.

"Princess Innozia. The Mathra are likely to avoid us if we make our way to sea water. I have set up base in an underwater lagoon. We must try and lure this ship as close to the coast as possible before other Mathra ships find out we have stopped them from killing the president," Mogoma said to Innozia via communication device.

The Andromedan soldiers began retreating. The Mathra followed after them as they headed toward the Hawaan forest. Menzi wondered what Mogoma's plan was, much less whether it would work.

*Location: Hawaan Forest, South Africa*

Menzi, Innozia, Nammid, Smeggar and other soldiers of the Andromedan army sped through the Hawaan forest trying to avoid the attack ships of the Mathra. They hoped that the trees of the forest would shield them from the view and attack of the combat vehicle.

A field of white African Dog Roses was nearby. The flowers swayed back and forth violently under the force of the Mathra attack ships. Dark clouds gathered in the sky and Durban turned as dark as evening.

Mogoma flew slightly above them, holding the positive Logos in a protective orb as flying ahead of him. Mogoma dared not turn around, lest he lose focus and unwittingly surrender the positive Logos to the Mathra.

Menzi's chest began to burn from the sheer exhaustion of running for hours. But he could not stop running. Mogoma and the others were well ahead of him, as expected, given that they were beings of heightened abilities.

He often forgot that he was also a Nommos like Mogoma. However Mogoma had the benefit of knowing his whole life that he was a Nommos. Mogoma was also much taller than Menzi was. Menzi still struggled with many of his newfound abilities.

He looked up to the sky and saw Taheeq shooting psionic blasts at the smaller Mathra drones which were also in hot pursuit of them and the positive Logos. He knew that Taheeq was powerful, but could only hold them back for so long.

Suddenly Menzi's scales began to glow in a bright amber colour and he began to levitate. His eyes began to glow as well. His subconscious mind began to take over and he shot to Taheeq's aid in fighting off the Mathra assault drones.

Some of the small assault drones were taken down by Mogoma's shots. However, whenever one Mathra assault drone was taken down, another three seemed to rise to take its place.

More Mathra crafts were coming in the direction of the chase. The Mathra assault crafts began shooting at the Andromedan soldiers. Innozia's craft went down first. She managed to eject herself from it before it crashed on the ground.

Mogoma veered down to make sure the princess was okay. He landed the Nommos ship that he, Menzi and the positive Logos were in. He hopped out and tended to the princess. Menzi reluctantly hopped out after him carrying the positive Logos in his arms.

"Erm...Mogoma, what's happening? I thought the plan was to get out of the way of the danger. I'm not an expert on these things, but from where I'm looking it looks like we're sitting ducks at the moment," Menzi said, failing to hide his frantic anxiety.

Mogoma did not answer Menzi. The Mathra ships began circling above them, much like vultures over a dying animal in the desert. Menzi helped Innozia up. She gave no word of thanks but looked up at the Mathra ships that were now surrounding them. More Andromedan soldiers landed their crafts and stood alongside the princess.

They pulled their weapons out and began firing at the many Mathra ships hovering above them with sinister intent. One of the Mathra ships sent a shot back that made the shooting Andromedan soldiers squat for cover. The shot shook the ground like a minor tremor.

"Okay, Mogoma. You're going to have to keep it real with me now. I promise I won't get mad. On a scale of one to ten, how screwed are we?" Menzi said to Mogoma. The force of the Mathra craft engines blew on the group like a vile gust of wind.

Menzi struggled to maintain his balance as the wind blew. He held on to the positive Logos in his arms even tighter. The Mathra craft began to take aim at the group. The suspension of the moment suggested the death blow was on its way.

Menzi fell to his knees, almost as if to begin a prayer. A large ball of light descended from the largest Mathra ship towards the soldiers. Menzi's eyes dilated as his jaw dropped.

Suddenly the positive Logos began to levitate out of his hands. He tried to hold on to it but it was drawn to the air by a pull stronger than magnetic attraction. The Andromedans looked up at the positive Logos as it continued floating in the air.

The baby still looked as though it was asleep. It opened its eyes and an orange glow shot out. The baby turned around, still levitating, until it was facing the Mathra ships directly.

The little baby raised its hands, almost as if it were reaching out to a parent to pick it up. A large, destructive green orb was inching closer and closer to the Andromedans. The positive Logos levitated in front of the orb, unfazed by immediate danger it posed.

A blue light began to form from the palms of the positive Logos. In the blink of an eye, the positive logos destroyed all the Mathra ships in sight. Mathra ships got torn to shreds, burnt down and others wasted into non-existence at the sheer force of the positive Logos' power.

The Andromedan soldiers hid their faces from the brilliant and blinding light of the sonic wave. It took more than three minutes for the light to die down. When they looked up there was not a single Mathra ship in the sky waiting to attack them.

The positive Logos gently landed back in Menzi's arms. He looked at the baby amazed at what it just did. He looked to Mogoma, as if to demand an explanation for what he just witnessed.

"You didn't tell me it could do that. So, if that was the case, why could we just send this little one to deal with the bad guys and leave it at that? Surely that would have been easier and less dangerous?" Menzi asked.

"Yes, sometimes the positive Logos is known to exhibit some fascinating traits, including self awareness and free will. However, these are not displayed consistently and cannot be trusted to show themselves in your favour every time. That is why we need to protect it," Mogoma explained.

141

Menzi's eyes cocked open, almost as if he had an embarrassing epiphany. Innozia climbed over a tree stump so that she stood taller than all of her soldiers, except for the massive Smeggar.

"Soldiers, today we were fortunate that the positive Logos assisted us. We cannot expect that to happen next time or ever again. I have signaled to our commonwealth in Andromeda that we need more support over to assist us. Until they arrive, we need to head back to our base camp in the south and lay low. We cannot take the Mathra on as we are now," she said.

"We accomplished two important missions. We managed to locate the positive logos and we protected the President of your nation, Kwataar. From now on, we need to be on our guard. The Mathra are not defeated yet. More ships are out there and when they discover what we have done to this fleet, they will come after us with everything they have," Mogoma said.

Menzi looked down at the positive Logos and up at Mogoma again. He looked around at the soldiers of the Andromedan army.

"Are you willing to fight on our side, young Nommos," Mogoma asked as he extended his hand to Menzi.

Menzi looked at Mogoma's hand and nodded slowly to himself before grabbing Mogoma's palm. "I'm ready to fight on your side."


## EPILOGUE

Minister of State Security Bongani Dladla walked through the dark corridors of the west wing offices at the Union Buildings. Flanked by two bodyguards on either side, they walked with an unmistakable urgency.

They turned a corner as presidential security guards stood watching them pass. They arrived at President Hlongwane's office. He sat at his desk in a revolving chair that faced the wall, away from the door.

"President, thank you for agreeing to see me. This is a pressing time, perhaps more so than any other time in our democratic government. We are getting calls from the White House, The Kremlin, the British Crown, the Chinese, Delhi, everyone," the minister said.

"That is understandable. We cannot even begin to make sense of the past few weeks for ourselves. How do we explain what has happened to the leaders of the free world? I'm not even sure I believe, never mind understand, what I've seen with my own eyes," the

143

president answered, his chair still facing away from the minister.

"What should we do, president? We need to know! Our intelligence corps are telling us that these leaders want to hold a meeting in New York about this. I won't go back to them without a directive from you," Dladla insisted.

The president did not respond. The minister was slightly agitated. "President, please turn around and look at me, at least. With all due respect, I don't think you appreciate the seriousness of this situation," the minister pleaded.

The president's chair revolved slowly until he was facing the minister and his guards. President Hlongwane's face had a vacant expression, which gave no hints of fear or concern. He sat up and rested his elbows on his desk.

"I am very much aware of the seriousness of the situation. But we have lost but one life. Our responses to the situation have been found to be the best possible option and our investigations will find the cause of the problem," President Hlongwane retorted.

Dladla retreated. "My apologies, Mr. President. I did not mean to second guess your authority or your regard for the nation. I am just under tremendous pressure. Shall I give the green light for these meetings and arrange for us to go to New York?" Dladla asked.

Hlongwane looked Dladla straight in the eye, with a serious scowl. "It's early days. Do what you feel is right. We are going to go to the New York meeting. We are continuing to investigate what's happening, but we cannot attack an enemy we do not know," Hlongwane said.

"What does that mean, President? Do we tell the army to hold their fire? Does this have to do with what you saw when you had that encounter? Please tell me, President. We need to know," Dladla pleaded.

"For now, I will say this. I think we know exactly who our enemy is now. Your orders will be given to you in due course. And once you get your orders, our army will attack the identified enemy and will not hold back until they are completely destroyed," Hlongwane said.

Hlongwane revolved his chair until he had his back turned to the minister and his guards once again. As he turned he grabbed a glass of amber ale on the desk. Dladla could see that he had already taken a sip from the glass.

"Thank you President. Thank you for your faith in me. I will follow your orders exactly as you have given them. I will not let you down. When we find out who our enemies are, we will not stop attacking them until they are destroyed completely," Dladla said as he nervously twisted his fingers and bowed his head sheepishly.

The minister left the office of the president. His guards followed him out. Hlongwane sat alone in his office responding to Dladla's pledge of loyalty and allegiance.

Hlongwane's eyes turned green with a menacing glow as an evil smile broke on his face. His face turned pitch black and appendages peered out from his back as he laughed to himself, all alone in his office.

"I know you won't let me down, minister. And we will destroy our enemies. We will destroy them until they are all gone. After all...all things burst into flames and crumble into ashes. But the smoke rises to the stars," he said to himself.

*To Be Continued...*

## ABOUT THE AUTHOR

Khulekani Magubane is a journalist and author from Estcourt, KwaZulu Natal. He has been writing published books since 2004. He currently works in Cape Town as a journalist. He enjoys travelling, writing and story telling. He has been invited to literary events including the 2014 Time of The Writer in Durban, the Cape Town Book Fair in 2012 and the Storymoja Book Festival in Nairobi, Kenya in 2015.

## ABOUT THE BOOK

Awkward and timid youngster Menzi Gumede finds himself the unlikely hero of planet earth and the universe as we know it. An evil empire bent on destroying the entire universe and reforming it in its own image has descended upon earth and means mankind no good. Menzi and his newfound friends must protect earth and ensure that the evil Mathra Empire do not get their claws on the positive Logos. Our heroes cannot fail or they along with everything they know will be wiped out.

Printed in the United States
by Baker & Taylor Publisher Services